KENS

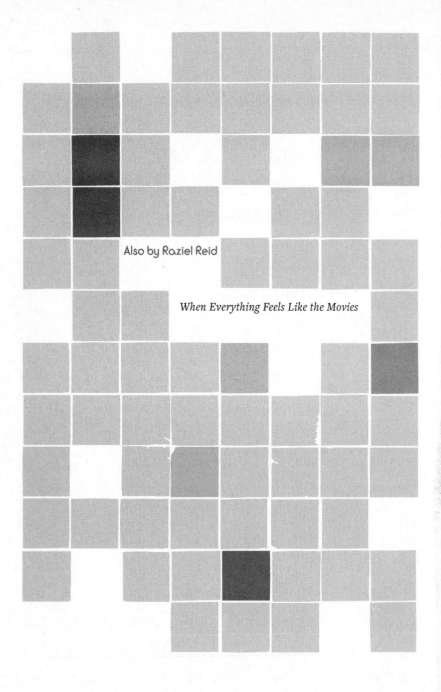

Also by Raziel Reid

When Everything Feels Like the Movies

KENS

RAZIEL REID

PENGUIN TEEN

an imprint of Penguin Random House Canada Young Readers,
a Penguin Random House Company

First published 2018

1 2 3 4 5 6 7 8 9 10 (LSC)

Manufactured in the U.S.A.

Library and Archives Canada Cataloguing in Publication
Reid, Raziel, 1990-, author
     Kens / Raziel Reid.
Issued in print and electronic formats.
ISBN 978-0-7352-6377-2 (hardcover).—ISBN 978-0-7352-6378-9 (EPUB)

     I. Title.
PS8635.E435K46 2018   C813'.68   C2017-905750-2
                                               C2017-905751-0

Library of Congress Control Number: 2018930583

www.penguinrandomhouse.ca

Penguin
Random House
PENGUIN TEEN CANADA

KENS GLOSSARY

Bae

1. Version of *babe* used by people who have a false sense of coolness.

   "Bae is gonna be all mine while his girlfriend is recovering from having her wisdom teeth pulled."

Baphomet

1. Depicted in Aleister Crowley's *Magick* (*Book 4*) as a divine androgyne and "the hieroglyph of arcane perfection."
2. A demon identified in conspiracy-analysis videos on YouTube as being inconspicuously present in pop culture photographs, movies and music videos.

Basics

1. People with common taste and behavior.

   Basic: *"I shop at H&M and just paid my taxes!"*

Bih

1. *Bitch* for lazy hipster faggots.

Bye Felicia

1. Goodbye and good riddance. "Felicia" is a person no one cares about.

   "Lady Gaga said she's quitting music to focus on acting . . . 'Bye Felicia!'"

2. A phrase coined in the stoner comedy film *Friday*.

Everything

1. Used as an adjective to describe something worthy of worship.

   "Your Brazilian butt lift is EVERYTHING."

Extra

1. Excessive, unnecessary, over-the-top.

   "Her latest mental breakdown was some extra shit!"

Fosh

1. A derivative of *for sure*, which evolved in street vernacular as *fo sho*, eventually being shortened to *fosh*.

Gagging

1. Shocked, mesmerized, impressed. Used when something is so fierce you can't help but gag over the fabulosity of it all.

Gur

1. Version of *girl* originated by gangsters but most often used by suburban white girls.

   "I don't know, gur, I think Orlando's penis is bigger than Justin's."

Hella

1. Originated in the Bay Area, *hella* is commonly used in place of *really* or *very* when describing something.

   "Poor people are hella gross."

2. Supplemental; infers a great quantity of something, or its success.

    "I made hella bills on that pole."

3. An affirmation.

    Ken 1: *"I'm, like, so skinny."*

    Ken 2: *"Hella."*

Hunty

1. An amalgam of *honey* and *cunty*.

2. A colloquialism affectionately used amongst the drag queen community.

    "Your performance was on point tonight, hunty!"

Kiki

1. A small get-together/party almost always involving vodka.

    "Math class is tough. Let's have a kiki instead."

Lit

1. Turned up.

    "Aspen was lit."

2. Intoxicated.

    "I was so lit for first period."

Living

1. To love the moment or thing.

    "I'm LIVING for his nude Snapchats."

Reading

1. Clever and bitchy judgments.

2. The act of pointing out a flaw in someone else, exaggerating it and publicly shaming them.

3. It's, like, an art.

Spill the tea

1. Divulge. A term started within the gay community of San Antonio, Texas, inspired by the idea of having old Southern tea parties filled with gossip.

Thirsty

1. An individual who is desperate for attention or approval. Examples include:
   - *an Instagram account filled with nothing but selfies*
   - *that guy who hits on every girl in a group of friends*
   - *celebrities who tip off the paparazzi before going to Starbucks*

Thot

1. An acronym for That Hoe Over There; commonly used in the wrong context to describe someone trashy.
   Correct usage: *"Thot thinks she's going to be set for life if she gets knocked up by the reality star."*
   Incorrect usage: *"That chick is such a thot; I can totally see her tampon string hanging out of her mini-skirt!"*
2. A contemptible person.

'Zif

1. Abbreviation of *as if*, meaning "Yeah right."
   Peasant: *"Hey, Ken, wanna go on a date to Dreamhouse this weekend?"*
   Ken: *"'Zif!"*

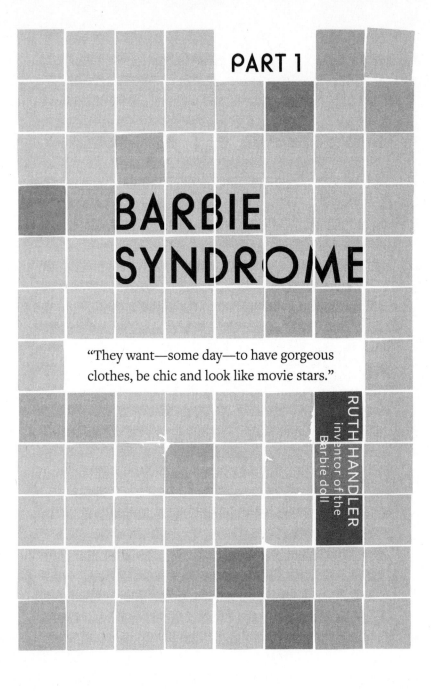

PART 1

BARBIE SYNDROME

"They want—some day—to have gorgeous clothes, be chic and look like movie stars."

RUTH HANDLER
inventor of the
Barbie doll

MAGIC EARRING

The gym class runs laps in unison.

The Kens are flawless. Ken Hilton, in baby-pink short-shorts and white socks pulled up to his knees, is at the helm. No one runs faster than him: not Ken Roberts, who wouldn't dare, but not even Ken Carson, who is technically the jock Ken.

There are minor differences in each Ken, but they're all made from the same face sculpt. Literally. Ken Hilton's dad is a plastic surgeon, and they have each been created from the same mold, with nothing much distinguishing them from their tiny plastic muse. Except that the Ken doll has more humanity. If the Kens were their own Disney movie (the first Disney movie ever to be rated R), then Ken Hilton would be the evil queen, Ken Roberts would be the princess and Ken Carson would be Prince Charming. Willows High is their kingdom.

Willows High is the prettiest school in Willows, Wisconsin. It looks more like a luxury department store than a school, with classrooms that could be display windows (Hermès throws over the backs of desks in case you catch a chill, lighting from the sides of the room and *never* from directly above to avoid unflattering shadows), and a student body more accessorized than mannequins. It's located in the exclusive Willows Hills neighborhood, a.k.a. The Hills.

The Hills looks like a higher dimension. The sun shines at an eternally positive angle to fair Venus off the topiary (doll heads, unicorns, atomic bombs) visible on the sprawling boulevards. Glass-box mansions jut from the hillside and glisten; infinity pools spill through time. All of Willows is pristine. Days pass as if choreographed and designed. If you go out far enough, eventually you'll hit a wall. Down on the Mainland, which is what everyone calls the neighborhood surrounding The Hills where last season lives, sit row after row of dollhouses on streets so polished you can see your reflection. Each house has a dog, a white-picket fence and porcelain flowers in the garden.

Tommy can feel his breath getting shorter as he runs, and he blinks through a bead of sweat dripping from his eyebrow, imagining an inexplicable gust of wind blowing through the gym, messing everyone's hair but leaving the Kens' perfectly styled.

Kens only use Dippity-Do gel; they order it by the gallon (and Ken Roberts even has a tramp-stamp tattoo of the logo). Ken-hair always looks like a part of their immaculately toned body, an extension of synthetic gold flesh. The Kens never sweat. No matter how much a Ken exerts himself (for example, ripping tags off designer clothes, holding up a diamond to a loupe, double-fisting double vodkas), he doesn't perspire. He just gets a little extra sheen. Like he's brand new. Straight out of Satan's doll factory.

Soul sold separately.

"Could Ken Hilton's shorts be any shorter?" Allan puffs on his inhaler.

"If a teste isn't hanging out they're not shorts," Tommy says. "That's Ken 101."

Some say it's their blog, SoFamous.tumblr.com—home to celebrity gossip and merciless student-body rumors—that elevated the Kens past the established high-school nobility: the jocks and their bitch kids of Instagram girlfriends.

But Tommy always thought it was the butt implants.

@KenHilton
666k followers   0 following

Ken Hilton has a private account—not that he's discreet about anything. He has one of his minions curate his profile to ensure he maintains 666k followers at all times. There are thousands rumored to be on the waiting list, including Tommy. Always the requested, never the verified.

Tommy and Ken Hilton go way back. Tommy knows his real last name! It's more dangerous than saying *Voldemort*. Ken Hilton even makes his parents use Hilton.

They were friends at school in grade one. The summer before second grade, Tommy and Ken Hilton were at camp together. Tommy had the biggest crush on their youth counselor, Derek, who evoked the eggplant emoji in swim trunks. But Ken Hilton decided he wanted Derek for himself.

The drama queen would pretend to be drowning in the lake just to be rescued by Derek, or at night he'd scream and jump out of his sleeping bag into Derek's tan biceps because he thought he felt a spider. It worked. Derek was so consumed with Ken Hilton's needs that Tommy was invisible to him. And if Derek did show him any attention, Ken Hilton found a way to come between them.

One night around the campfire when Derek was helping Tommy make a s'more, Ken Hilton swung the flaming marshmallow off the end of his stick right at him. It landed on Tommy's cheek and left him with a small burn scar. Derek blamed Ken Hilton for being careless, and Ken Hilton blamed Tommy for being a cock block.

Shortly after camp, Ken Hilton blocked Tommy. He'd been replaced.

@KenRoberts
1.1m followers   1,762 following

Ken Roberts is captain of the cheer squad and queen of Instagram. Okay, so he bought a million of his followers. He still gets asked by various fashion labels to post ads modeling their clothes. His feed is all ruffled pink crop-tops that say "Daddy" across the chest.

Tommy remembers Ken Roberts pre-factory, when he was named Evan. The shy, chubby kid who sat at the back of the class and ate paper. Ken Hilton tormented

him relentlessly before dropping Tommy and introducing his new toy to a life of selfies and starvation.
Evan had mousy hair and baby cheeks and a horse
named Dancer. He loved all animals. But that changed
when he became Ken: Fur Fag Edition.

He's still into horses. Or at least horse tranquilizers.

@KenCarson
450k followers   376 following

Ken Carson is in the closet. He's straight! Tutti told
Tommy that she caught him going down on Francie
Fairchild in the girls' locker room.

When Ken Carson moved from Malibu to Willows
for sophomore year he was a tan surfer dude with a
hot car, so he was hella confused as to why he wasn't
more popular. Even when he upped his steroid intake
and was made tight end for the Barks, Willows High's
football team, he didn't hold the same rank he had at
his old school. He learned that at Willows High if the
Kens don't receive you, you're nobody.

Ken Carson knew what he had to do if he wanted to
rule. He had to go gay for slay!

(You have to be gay to be a Ken. They're of the one
and ten percent.)

Soon after sending Ken Hilton nudes and meeting
him under the bleachers, he was in.

The gym class stops running laps when Ken Hilton makes a scene.

"I lost my earring!" he gasps, clutching his ear, which is allegedly the last real part of his body.

Ken Carson relaxes his glutes. "Dude, no way!"

"I'm going to kill myself," Ken Hilton cries, his tears matching his crocodile sneakers.

"What are you waiting for?" Ken Roberts shrieks at the rest of the class. "Find Ken Hilton's diamond or even more blood will spill for it!" Ken Roberts is higher pitched than Truman Capote. Not that the Kens know who Truman Capote is. They may eat breakfast at Tiffany's, but books aren't for reading—they're for snorting lines off of.

The students scan the floor. Tommy and Tutti get on all fours, hoping they will be the one to find Ken Hilton's earring. Allan crouches down but doesn't really look. He rolls his eyes behind his round-lens glasses. While Tutti is the Kens' number one fan girl, and Tommy is a total masochist for their approval, Allan has no respect for the Kens. He thinks they're evil, and he thinks being evil is a bad thing.

"What does it even look like?" Allan asks.

"It's a pink stud," Tutti says. "Ken Hilton alone can give pink the nerve of red."

The Kens wear an earring in their left ear like Earring Magic Ken, the Mattel doll they model themselves after. Earring Magic Ken was the first gay Ken. Unofficially. He appeared on shelves in the early 1990s wearing a purple leather Gaultier vest over a mesh tank top. His outfit came complete with a chrome cock ring necklace. Mattel insisted it wasn't a cock ring, but it so obviously was. Earring Magic Ken looked like the stereotypical gay guy of the era you'd find dancing under a disco ball, blinded by strobe lights. He was quickly discontinued. To the Kens, he's the ideal. Plastic and controversial. They made an effigy of his mannequin head, and burn Kellys in his name.

Ken Roberts and Ken Carson twerk around the gym pretending to look for the lost earring. Ken Hilton, meanwhile, buries his face in the jersey of Barks quarterback Brad Curtis.

"Don't worry, bae." Brad kisses Ken Hilton's platinum crown. "I'll find it for you."

"I still can't get over Ken Hilton turning Brad," Tutti whispers as she and Tommy watch Brad join the search. "He and Francie were going to be homecoming king and queen!"

"Until Ken Hilton decided a BBD was the must-have accessory of the season," Tommy quips.

"A what?" Allan asks.

"Urban Dictionary that shit."

The gym door swings open. A tall, dark and handsome doll enters wearing a black leather jacket and boots crusted with mud. His untied laces whip from side to side as he slowly walks through the maze of crawling students. He stops at half-court and leans over to pick something up off the floor. It glimmers between his fingers.

"Who is *that*?" Tutti asks.

The guy walks right up to where Ken Hilton is standing. Tommy watches nervously. Engaging with Ken Hilton is more formal than engaging with the Queen. You have to bend the knee *and* kiss his ass while you're down there, and then he may dignify you with oral—speech, that is—but most likely he'll give you a dirty look, pretend to be talking to someone on his iconic pink-rhinestone iPhone, and wave you away like an unattractive guy at Dreamhouse, the Kens' favorite nightclub.

But Ken Hilton's lips spread into a smile as he looks the new kid up and down with a day-drunk flicker of his glossy blue eyes. "You're hot," he says. "And not just because you're holding eight carats."

DON'T EAT

Three Kens walk up to a lunch counter . . .

A lunch lady scurries to the back to retrieve the caviar Ken Hilton has specially ordered. Ken Roberts has already purged three bowls of chili and is back for more. Another lunch lady plops a steaming heap of chili onto Ken Carson's tray and warns him it's hot. But he assumes she's calling *him* hot. He puts a huge spoonful in his mouth and his eyes well with tears.

Tommy, Allan and Tutti are waiting in line behind the Kens. Tutti hurries to the counter and passes Ken Carson a napkin.

Ken Carson spits out the burning mouthful of chili and passes the napkin back to her.

"Thanks, dude." He smiles. A veneer literally sparkles.

Ken Roberts looks over at them and gasps. "Your outfit is savage as fuck," he says, lifting his iPhone to take a photo for the "Look of the Day" section on SoFamous. It's almost always a Ken.

Tommy momentarily thinks Ken Roberts is talking to him, but of course not; Tommy can't afford the designer stores that plaster the Kens' feeds. He shops at Zara for knock-offs. Tutti comforts him by saying it's very Duchess of Cambridge.

"*So* trust-fund hipster," Ken Roberts tells a bewildered Allan, who looks behind him to see who Ken Roberts is talking to.

Allan is wearing a graphic tee that says "Books Make Me Happy, You Not So Much" tucked into brown corduroy pants that have been cut rather jaggedly at the bottom to show off a few inches of his bright blue dinosaur-print socks. Allan is one of the few students at Willows High to so openly defy the Kens' consumer culture.

The Kens stride off to the table at the center of the cafeteria where they sit with the Barks football players and the cheer squad.

Ken Hilton is the most popular Ken because his first nose was most people's third nose, but Ken Carson has all the boys dangling from his impressive foreskin. He's taller, broader and a stronger football player. The jocks at Willows High have a particular respect for all the Kens, whom they treat like otherworldly creatures. Mostly, they're in awe because the Kens have control of the girls in a way the jocks only do when they've spiked their drinks.

Ken Roberts is a feminist icon because he hasn't digested food since the second grade. Plus, Harry Styles DM'd him (and, according to Ken Roberts, DP'd him with Ken Carson). His skinny twink figure can rock runway fashion better than anyone. The shallow girls of Willows High worship him.

Tutti holds up the napkin filled with Ken Carson's mouthful of food.

"I think it's love," she says.

"Are you still holding that?" Allan asks.

Tutti ditches the napkin in the trash bin for her own self-respect. They get their lunch and go over to their usual table in the corner of the caf, occasionally co-inhabited with random art freaks.

"Hey, Tommy," Tutti says as she sits across from him and Allan. "I need a male model for a drag tutorial I'm doing. Any plans after school?"

Tommy is distracted by Blaine entering the cafeteria. That's the name of the newest product at Willows High, which Tommy learned in Spanish class. Francie and fellow cheerleader Midge were gossiping about meeting him. Unfortunately, Tommy didn't have any morning classes with Blaine.

Allan follows Tommy's line of vision. He waves his hand in front of Tommy's face. "Earth to Tommy," he says.

"I hear he drives a Harley." Tutti gives Blaine a once-over. "Guys on motorcycles are so sexy." She turns back to Tommy. "So what do you say? If you can't, then I'm making Allan do it."

"Kill me," Allan says. "Wait, I'm working tonight. Sorry, Toots!"

Allan works at Taco Accessory in the food court at Willows Mall. Tommy doesn't get it, but Allan won't take money from his parents. They tried to buy him a BMW for his birthday, but he refused it and bought a beat-up second-hand car with his savings instead. He wants to pave his own way or something equally esoteric. His whole family is weird.

They may live up in The Hills but they're total hippies. His mom only gets Botox once a year.

"Don't feed the model," Tommy finally answers Tutti, pushing his tray of chili across the table. He keeps one eye on Blaine, who is leaning against the cafeteria counter waiting for the lunch lady to dish out his chili. Tommy isn't the only one who's noticed him.

Ken Hilton rises from his spot at the center table and struts to the counter. His arm grazes Blaine's leather jacket and he sticks out his butt. Ken Hilton has a permanent arch in his lower back. He makes his plastic surgeon father experiment on him all the time. He has, like, no ribs.

Over at the center table, Brad cracks his knuckles as he watches Ken Hilton lean over Blaine to seductively grab a spoon. Tommy can't help but notice.

Ken Hilton turns and walks back to his table in a perfectly straight line, one leg in front of the other, fully aware that Blaine is watching.

Brad nudges his buddy Todd, who is cute but stupid in a varsity jacket. Linebacker of the Barks. They jump up from the table and make their way over to Blaine.

Todd puts his finger in Blaine's chili and swirls it around. He licks his finger. "This stuff runs right through me, man. You ever have that problem?"

"This town looks like it rains Pepto-Bismol," Blaine says. "How could anyone have that problem?"

"You calling him a liar?" Brad shoves Blaine's chest, knocking his bowl of chili onto the floor.

"Heathens." Blaine takes a deep breath through his nose.

He's still inhaling when Brad puts him in a headlock, pushing him to his knees while Todd lifts his leg and farts in his face.

"Yep," Todd says. "That was a wet one."

Brad lets go and high-fives Todd. They start barking, and once they get going, all the Barks at the center table join in. Soon the whole cafeteria is barking.

The cafeteria instantly shuts the fuck up when Blaine pulls a gun out of his leather jacket and points it at Brad and Todd. They put up their hands.

"Shit, man," Brad says. "We're sorry. We didn't realize you're Muslim!"

"I'm a colonial." Blaine gives them a dirty look. He pulls the trigger.

The gun clicks.

"Relax, ladies." Blaine presses the barrel to the side of his head and pulls the trigger. The gun clicks again. "It's a camera," he says. "Captures the look on a person's face when they think it's about to be blown off."

Blaine taps the gun on Todd's head.

"See," he says. "As light as you."

Tommy watches as Blaine tucks the camera gun in his jacket, steps over his spilled lunch and casually strolls out of the cafeteria.

"Fake or not," he hears Allan muttering next to him. "That just isn't appropriate in today's climate."

BEAT THE FACE

The makeup photos Tutti posts on Instagram have a large following. She's really good. Tommy is her frequent test-subject. They're up in her room, Tommy sitting in front of a mirror surrounded by small lightbulbs. A printed photo of Tommy and Tutti fooling around with the Face Swap app is tucked into the frame.

The drag look Tutti is doing on him for her latest shoot is in honor of Ken Hilton, who will be performing as his drag alter ego, Sandy Hooker, at the Willows High homecoming game tomorrow afternoon.

Ads for the game are spammed all over SoFamous. While Tutti is beating his face, Tommy scrolls through the Tumblr. The Kens know all. They're illuminated with secrets and forbidden knowledge (celebrity dick sizes, Lucky Blue Smith's iCloud password, et cetera).

"Play the song," Tutti tells Tommy. "Maybe I'll edit it in as background music on this Story."

"Watch Ken Hilton sue you for copyright," Tommy says.

"That'd be extra." Tutti reaches over and presses Play on Tommy's phone.

Sandy Hooker dropped a single. It's called "Hunty." Ken Hilton sings the lines with a sultry voice filtered through heavy Auto-Tune over a pounding house beat.

They call me hunty | You give I like to get | Don't call me cunty | When I be making you wet | They call me hunty | I can be so sweet | But I mix my honey | With shit from the street

Ken Hilton's father, Dr. Hilton, bought him a music video production for his second sweet-sixteen birthday party. (Terrified of becoming an aging twink, he decided to be sixteen for another year.) In the video Ken Hilton is wearing nothing but pink dental floss.

The track plays and Tommy keeps scrolling, landing on an item about Willows High's newest student. There's a photo of Blaine making a goofy face for the camera, sticking out his tongue, bulging his eyes. It's like he's purposely trying to make himself look as bad as possible, which is unprecedented at Willows High, where everyone tries to be as perfect as the Kens. If you're lucky enough to have your photo taken in the hall and posted to SoFamous, you're usually giving red carpet realness.

The only text in the post is, "Remember school rules, gurs: a Ken goes first. Even if it is ISIS! xo."

Tutti reads the post over Tommy's shoulder.

"I wonder what his story is," she says. "He's so mysterious."

When Blaine pulled the camera gun, Tommy took in Ken Hilton's reaction: he was shocked. And it isn't easy to shock

Ken Hilton, who lives to provoke. He brought the contents of his first colonic in a jar for show and tell as a kid. Tommy can tell Blaine has piqued Ken Hilton's curiosity, and when Ken Hilton wants something, he bends the universe until it brings it to him on a pink slide.

Tutti lifts a makeup brush to Tommy's nose. He looks up from his phone and examines his reflection in her mirror. "Even with contour my nose is so *big*," he says. "It's the bane of my existence."

"Your nose is adorable. It has character."

"It has several."

"You have to stop comparing yourself to the Kens. You know they're totally manufactured. The Bride of Wildenstein is their spirit animal."

Tommy touches the scar on his cheek from summer camp with Ken Hilton. It has faded over the years, but there's a small patch of skin that looks as fine as wrinkled tissue paper.

"I have just the foundation." Tutti puts her hand on his shoulder and gives it a squeeze.

"Ken Hilton's dead eyes are definitely set on Blaine," Tommy says. "His first day at Willows High and he's already been featured on SoFamous. They've never given me a headline."

"You can find me in the archive under 'Two-Ton Tutti.' It's not that glamorous."

"Just because the Kens say your pink scale should be permanently set to 110 pounds doesn't mean everyone has to obey," Tommy says.

He watches Tutti covering his scar. "I just can't help but feel like they're ignoring me on purpose."

In first grade, when Tommy and Ken Hilton were friends, he'd always have to play at Ken Hilton's house. Ken Hilton couldn't leave The Hills because the Mainland made him itchy. They'd have a lot of fun hiding Ken Hilton's mom's pill bottles around the house and watching her throw cushions off the couch as she looked for them, desperate to re-up. Barbara Hilton is a pilled-out Willows landmark. Imagine all of the Restylane and Juvéderm in the faces of Bravo's *Real Housewives* being molded into a human being and you get Barbie Hilton. She's posted on SoFamous every time she gets another DUI, is arrested for public intoxication/battery of a police officer or checks in to rehab. So, daily.

Ken Hilton was always really advanced. He'd mock Tommy when Tommy was afraid to try the pills they were hiding from Barbie, and it had been his idea that he and Tommy should *finally* come out together in tagged Facebook posts.

But then, a day earlier than planned, Ken Hilton did it without him. He wrote a post and didn't tag Tommy. It went viral. He got so much attention for it. Everyone called him brave. A real pioneer.

Tommy was hurt and confused, especially when Ken Hilton ignored him on the playground. He was too busy signing autographs from his adoring public.

The next day, Tommy decided to come out alone. When he came down for breakfast that morning, his mom put her hand on her hip and tilted her head.

"Are you jealous of all the attention your friend is getting?" she asked.

"No!" Tommy insisted. "I really am gay!"

"Oh, Tommy." His mom waved him off. "You wish."

Ken Hilton's coming-out post got thousands of Likes. Tommy's only got one—from the class "fire-crotch," as Ken Hilton called him during his ritualistic teasing. Allan.

That summer Tommy and Ken Hilton went to camp together, and after that, it was as if Tommy didn't exist in Ken Hilton's world. To this day, the Kens don't even write rumors about him on SoFamous, which they do for most people when they're bored. The Kens never claimed to be good people—or, in fact, to be people at all—but the meanest thing they've ever done is ignore Tommy.

"Face it." Tommy looks at Tutti through the mirror. "In a school where the Kens are queens who are treated like Queens, I'm the forgotten faggot. I'm brunette."

"We could dye it," Tutti suggests. Her hair is currently bright blue.

Tommy scrolls past the post about Blaine. The next post has been reblogged from the Willows High Stoner Conspiracy Theorists page. It's called "The Ken Conspiracy." Tommy presses Play.

"You want to know why they're so popular? They sold their souls, man," a Stoner Conspiracy Theorist says in the video, stopping to puff on a giant cross blunt. "Kens don't have actual blood in their veins. They have glitter. No one knows exactly how a commoner would join, but it's widely believed it would involve sacrificing your favorite maid and eating the organs of a drag queen."

"I haven't heard that one before." Tutti laughs.

Tommy looks back up at his reflection. With the makeup on and under the right light he's almost . . .
pretty.

POSSESSED DOLL

Streetlights brighten lawns of fluorescent-green grass, each blade as sharp as a surgeon's knife. The air is still and the sky is dark. Emerald leaves blow in the wind. A perfect storm is coming.

Tommy walks home from Tutti's house, his face tingling from the toner Tutti applied after taking off his makeup.

His parents are sitting in the living room holding a tablet between them when he walks through the door. They're watching InfoWars on YouTube.

"Oh, hi, Tommy!" his mom says. "Leftovers are in the fridge."

"Eat up," his father calls after him as Tommy starts climbing the stairs. "End times, son. End times."

The window is open inside his shoebox of a room. The only good thing about it is the small window with a view of the WILLOWSLAND sign across the hillside, framed far behind countless rooftops, winding roads and telephone poles. Tommy leans out of the window, staring longingly at the view, which is best at night when the hills are dark and the pink letters of the sign are lit up so bright they look like they're floating in the air.

It starts raining and Tommy closes the window. As he turns around, he sees himself in the mirror above his dresser. He runs his hand across his red and blotchy skin. The scar on his cheek looks more glaring than ever. And that's totally a zit about to surface on the tip of his nose.

He lifts his arms and tries to flex. What a joke. He's so lanky he makes Ken Roberts look like a heifer.

Tommy puts his face right up to the mirror and stares into his own eyes. It might just be the lightning outside, but it seems something is emerging in his pupil—a bulb, pulsating, as if on the cusp of a flash.

Falling back onto his bed, Tommy opens his computer and rewatches the Stoner Conspiracy Theorists' "Ken Conspiracy" video.

A gust of wind blows against the window. It rattles like a drug-addled heart. Branches scratch against the surface. Tommy's computer screen powers off and the room goes dark.

That night, Tommy can't sleep. He tosses and turns, his scar burning like it's new, the marshmallow still stuck to his skin. He kicks off his sheets. His mind won't turn off. If only he had a control panel.

He's thinking about the way Ken Hilton took the pink diamond stud from Blaine's hand so flirtatiously it was like they were exchanging bodily fluids. It made Tommy blush and stare down at the gym floor. He stayed on his hands and knees until Allan touched his arm and told him they could stop looking, crisis averted, Ken Hilton and his diamond had been reunited. The balance of the universe restored.

Tommy gives up on trying to sleep and gets out of bed, listening for any sound in the house. But his parents are logged out for the night. He sneaks into the dark hallway with a backpack slung over his shoulder; it holds his phone and one of his childhood Barbies. The Stoner Conspiracy Theorists said to bring Baphomet a gift of a virgin. Tommy could always offer himself—he's pretty sure he's destined to die one—but he's hoping Baphomet has a sense of humor.

He doesn't worry about the stairs creaking and waking his parents. Nothing creaks in Willows, except the Kens. And that's more of a squeak. It's the sexiest sound.

Down in the kitchen, he opens the liquor cabinet and looks through the bottles of liqueurs. Tommy's parents don't really drink anymore; ever since they joined a dispensary, they've become potheads. They're always at pro-legalization rallies. Fridays are Fried Days in the Rawlins household. Even his parents fit into trendy Willows better than he does. They're basically avatars.

Tommy manages to find a bottle of vodka at the back of the cabinet. It's only half full, but should do the trick . . . Tommy adds it to his bag, along with some candles he takes off of the dining room table. From the closet he pulls out the iRobot Roomba. His mom loves it so much she thinks it's a real maid. They even go grocery shopping together, Roomsy tidying up the aisles while his mom chats away with her other bestie, Siri.

Salt for the pentagram and ketchup to use in place of goat's blood. Tommy knows a farm on the outskirts of town that has goats, but since he doesn't have an actual maid to sacrifice, or the actual insides of a drag queen, maybe it'll be best if everything is fake.

According to the Kens, every bat of your eyelashes should be performative. And doesn't Tommy take sacrament when he goes to church with his mom and dad on Sundays? It's not the actual body of Christ. But you're supposed to pretend it is. Tommy's parents take him to Famous Family Church. Father Dude is the best show in town. He's even more dope than the pope. At Famous Family, old *Oprah Winfrey Show* transcripts are preached as gospel and *Us Weekly* is in the confessional booth. Tommy always feels so fresh after mass. Like a new post not yet defiled by the comments section.

It has stopped raining by the time Tommy steps outside. The street is even sleeker than usual. Thunder rolls in the sky. Tommy walks quickly down the middle of the deserted winding road toward the cemetery situated behind Famous Family.

Willows Forever is magical: the tombstones are chalk white and powdery, like they've all been coated with ivory cover-up. Fitting for the dead who were all cover girls. Jeff Koons topiary and sculptures are spread throughout the grounds, and the ghost of Narcissus haunts the large pond with floating pink water lilies.

Tommy walks deeper into the cemetery until he finds the clearing next to Bild Lilli's tomb, where the Stoners' video said to go. Bild Lilli was a shameless gold digger of German origin, a beauty queen and mistress of the first mayor of Willows. And the second. And the second mayor's son. In the photos of Bild Lilli you can find online, she has a curvy body and the face of a baby. The Kens idolize her.

Using the salt, Tommy makes a pentagram and places the Barbie in one of the points. He lights candles and pulls out Roomsy from his bag, then presses Record on his phone. Maybe if he submits the video to SoFamous the Kens will at least recognize his dedication.

Roomsy is thrown smack in the middle of the pentagram. Tommy kicks at the iRobot until it's shattered into pieces. Then he squirts the entire container of ketchup onto the offering and pulls out the bottle of vodka, taking a big swig and spitting it out. He's so ashamed. Kens swallow! But Tommy can't stand the taste. He pours the remaining vodka over Roomsy and Barbie. He just couldn't bring himself to kill an actual drag queen, and figures their insides would consist solely of vodka anyway.

"Baphomet, I summon you," Tommy says. He pulls out a lighter and uses the flame to ignite the vodka-soaked dust inside the crushed vacuum. Up it goes. "Make me a Ken and I'll be yours to play with forever!"

Tommy submits the video to SoFamous, just as a rumble spreads through the cemetery. Lightning sparks a cotton-ball cloud in the sky. Everything is whited out by the lights shining into Tommy's eyes.

PLASTIC PLACE

Robot embers glow in the grass. Tommy squints into the lights. He sees the shadowy frame of a body but can't quite distinguish a face. A candle blows out, sending smoke coiling around raindrops.

It thunders and starts to rain again. Tomorrow is going to be a slippery day in Willows. The streets will be like Lego in a bath.

The lights turn off and the rumbling goes quiet. When Tommy's eyes adjust to the dark, he can make out a parked motorcycle.

In a flash of lightning, a face.

"You," he says quietly.

"Making human sacrifices?" Blaine raises his eyes as he steps into the pentagram, the salt crunching under his boots.

Tommy is spared from answering by another roar of thunder.

"Kind of late for a motorcycle ride, isn't it?"

"Just trying to clear my head."

"Yeah, you and me both."

Tommy starts picking up the séance supplies from the ground, dropping them in his backpack. He can feel Blaine watching him as he picks up the Barbie. Some ketchup blood got on her arm. She looks like she slit her wrists.

"You go to Willows High, right?" Tommy asks, trying to play it cool.

"You go there?"

"I'm Tommy. We have P.E. together. You probably didn't notice me. I was on all fours . . . You're the guy who found the magic earring."

Blaine looks confused. Tommy smiles. He really is new.

"The pink diamond. Ken Hilton's. You know, the blond who doesn't look real."

"Reality is so fake it's TV," Blaine says.

Wax from a burning candle Tommy is holding drips onto his hand. He feels it harden. Blaine extinguishes the flickering flame between his fingers.

"If you're selling your soul, it's always best to start a bidding war." He arches his eyebrows like Jack Nicholson sticking his head through a door broken open with an ax.

Another flash of lightning. It gives Tommy a chill.

"Looks like it's gonna pour," Blaine says. "Want a ride home?"

Tommy drops the candle in his bag. "Anywhere but home."

The bike careens out of the cemetery. Tommy holds onto Blaine's wet leather jacket as they ride through the downpour. All of the lights are off in the houses they pass and the streets are empty. Everyone's safe inside, not only because it's so late but also because when it rains in Willows no one wants to risk water damage.

Blaine takes them to The Hills, pulling up to a chain-link fence surrounding a large cliff-side construction site. Blaine climbs the rattling fence.

"Plastic Place," he says. "Opening soon."

Blaine straddles the top and reaches down to give Tommy a hand up. They land in a muddy puddle on the other side. Tommy stares up at a massive concrete and glass structure.

"So this is the new mall," Tommy says. "I read about it on SoFamous."

"It's why my dad moved us here." Blaine leads him toward the building. "He's developing some properties in Willows. Thinks this place is some kind of utopia. I told him its own mayor called it a WASP country club on Swarovski-coated crack during a press conference, but that didn't seem to deter him."

They walk through an opening in the front of the building because the door hasn't yet been erected. The staircase in the entrance is the biggest Tommy has ever seen. It spirals for screen shot after screen shot.

Blaine jumps up the wooden treads two at a time. "You have to see this."

They go all the way up to the top floor, passing beams and a wide space that Blaine says will eventually be the food court. He leads Tommy down a long hallway with sawdust on the floor, construction supplies in the corner, pink insulation sticking out of the wall.

A door at the end of the hall takes them onto the roof. Tommy stares out at a panoramic view of Willows. It looks like a postcard with a photo taken using the Street View app. "And all that will be left of them are their Likes." He sighs.

"Nietzsche all on his mouth like liquor." Blaine smirks.

They climb even higher, up the ladder of the rooftop water tower. They're higher than the WILLOWSLAND sign—the ultimate billboard.

Street lamps emit the only light below. It's like the glow of a nightlight plugged into an outlet in a dark playroom, shining through the windows of the most intricate dollhouse ever made.

UNNATURAL SELECTION

Tommy gets a personal tour of the mall. The place is huge. Down in the basement is a storage room filled with row after row of shop mannequins with blond wigs. It's dark, but Blaine shines the light from his iPhone across the porcelain faces—deliberately blank, without a personality, so that you can project your dreams on them.

"Doll'icious," Tommy says.

Blaine kicks one over with the tip of his boot. It has a domino effect; an entire row of mannequins collapses and Tommy jumps out of the way.

The sun is starting to rise. There's no point in going home before school, so Blaine drives them to a diner to grab breakfast. Tommy tries to ask him questions about himself, but unlike most people in Willows, Blaine isn't especially eager to describe his design history.

"Where did you move from?" Tommy asks.

"Ohio."

"Do you live on the Mainland or The Hills?"

"Hills."

"Siblings?"

"Nope." Blaine squirts ketchup on his eggs, which reminds Tommy of the bloody Barbie in his backpack. "Which is surprising, considering my dad thinks grabbing them by the pussy is one of the Ten Commandments."

Tommy laughs. "You should meet *my* parents. Although you might want to download malware protection first."

After breakfast, they head to school. Tommy loves being on the back of Blaine's bike. He can't remember ever feeling so free. Sometimes life in Willows can feel like you're being moved from place to place, like an arm is extended from the sky and you're stuck in the grip of a hand with impeccable nail beds. But Blaine drives so fast the hand can't quite catch them.

They pull into the parking lot at Willows High. Tommy wishes he didn't have to get off.

Coach Summers's whistle blows. The Barks players are practicing on the field.

"You coming to the homecoming game after school?" Tommy asks. "I'm mostly going to see Ken Hilton's halftime performance. It'll make the Super Bowl look low-budget."

As if he only exists when being mentioned, Ken Hilton speeds into the parking lot in his pink Corvette convertible. Ken Roberts is in the passenger seat. Bubblegum pop blares from the speakers.

Ken Hilton is so consumed with his reflection in the rear-view mirror that he doesn't see Tommy standing at the end of Blaine's bike and almost drives straight into him. He comes to a screeching halt just as Blaine grabs Tommy's arm, pulling him out of the way.

"You, like, almost hit an animal!" Ken Roberts gasps.

Ken Hilton lowers his heart-shaped sunglasses. His eyes narrow on Blaine holding Tommy's arm.

"It looks rabid," he says, pushing his glasses up the ski-slope curve of his nose and speeding into a parking spot reserved for faculty only.

Principal Elliot lets the Kens get away with murder. Dr. Hilton funded the library, even though the Kens only read status updates. The whole faculty has been terrified of the Kens ever since a student teacher dared to object to Ken Hilton's sexual advances; Ken Hilton retaliated by having one of the tech geeks break into the poor guy's cloud and load it with his raunchiest selfies. Then Ken Hilton went to Principal Elliot and fake-cried for his life, saying the student teacher was soliciting him for photos. That student teacher was now Allan's manager at Taco Accessory.

Blaine finally lets go of Tommy's arm. "Try to stay alive." He heads toward the front steps of school, saying over his shoulder, "See ya at the game."

"Guess what?" Tutti is giddy as Tommy approaches her and Allan at the lockers. "I passed the Barks practicing on the field this morning and Ken Carson came up to me and asked if I had any black eyeliner. I guess the team ran out of Eye Black. Can you believe he knows I'm into makeup?"

"He probably follows your tutorials," Tommy says, dropping his backpack in his locker.

Tommy hates himself for it, but he's jealous. Tutti has her makeup posts, and Allan is a Science Geek of YouTube. At least he has a thing, even if it is posting tutorials on how to make a rocket from paper and straw. Half a million people want to learn how to do that!

If it weren't for Allan and Tutti, Tommy's not sure he could survive Impressions-obsessed Willows High. He and Allan became best friends in elementary, after Ken Hilton dropped Tommy. Before that, Ken Hilton had forbidden Tommy to talk to Allan because Allan had red hair, but Allan was the only one who was still nice to him even after Ken Hilton dropped him.

They became close with Tutti sophomore year. Ken Hilton tripped her right in the middle of the hallway one day and was filming with his iPhone as Ken Roberts tried to shove a toothbrush down her throat. Allan was fearless. He shoved Ken Roberts right off Tutti. The newest Ken, Ken Carson, displayed shocking chivalry by offering Tutti his hand and helping her off the floor.

After the Kens had strutted off, Tommy and Allan tried to console Tutti. Tommy pointed out that at least Ken Carson had touched her.

"Like that makes it okay!" Allan barked. But Tutti seemed to think it did. She remained devoted. It was like that time Justin Bieber spit on his fans from the balcony of his hotel. No matter how much the Kens degrade Tutti, she continues to worship. Tommy understands. The Kens have that effect on most people. It can't really be explained.

They turn the corner on the way to class, and Tutti is

still gushing about her run-in with Ken Carson this morning.

"His lips are so juicy," she's saying.

"Wait, isn't Eye Black a grease that's used to reduce the glare of sunlight when a player is on the field?" Allan asks. "It's supposed to be practical, not some kind of fashion statement."

"This is Ken Carson we're talking about." Tutti laughs. "He also asked if I had any cherry ChapStick."

Just as Tutti, Allan and Tommy pass the girls' bathroom, a bunch of girls run out, scared for their lives.

Before the door swings shut, Tommy catches a fleeting glimpse of Ken Hilton and Ken Carson in their element: touching up in front of the mirrors. Ken Hilton is at the center sink, as always. The bathroom light fixture is directly above his head, shining down on his blond. Ken Carson is sweaty from practice and is wearing a cropped football jersey. He's number 69.

Behind them, Ken Roberts is retching in one of the stalls. Ken Hilton surpasses the limitation of his Botox to look disgusted.

"I have no respect for bulimics," he says. "Anorexics are so much more disciplined."

Ken Roberts comes out of the stall, dabbing the corner of his mouth with a Benjamin Franklin.

"Let them puke cake." He sighs.

Ken Hilton turns to his carbon copies.

"Gurs," he says. "I have an idea."

"Dude, what?" Ken Carson asks.

Ken Roberts's eyes pop. "Do you need an emergency Botox shot?"

"What if we, like, introduced a new model?" Ken Hilton says. "Ken: Thot to Hot Edition."

Ken Carson counts on his fingers. "A fourth?"

"Why do we need another Ken?" Ken Roberts asks.

"So that all of Willows High will be confined to our hotbox. Oh, I'm bored and I need a project!" Ken Hilton runs a pink comb through his hair. "Lately, I've been finding extortion trite. Plus, I just added 'philanthropist' to my Twitter bio and I think it's important I not only tweet the talk but walk the walk. And not just down the runway of a charity fashion show. Even if I am a teenage model. IMG was, like, so wet for me that if my walk wasn't so fierce I would've slipped all over the place."

Ken Hilton only got the modeling contract because he knew he could. He'd never actually model. In his eyes, a model is nothing more than a glorified sales associate. They might as well be working at Willows Mall.

Introducing a fourth Ken to the market is Ken Hilton's chance to show consumers his power is truly omnipotent. That he can take a mere mortal and transform him into something supernal. Imagined by God. Reimagined by Ken Hilton! He's determined to prove to all of Willows High, and the greater viral world, that he is the ultimate creator. That he is better than God at creating glamour.

"I really want to do something positive for the world," he says. "Ugly people are so sad."

"Fosh," Ken Carson bobbles.

Ken Roberts huffs from a can of hairspray. "Who is she?"

"Thomas," Ken Hilton says. "Thomas Rawlins."

Ken Carson looks more confused than usual. "Dude, who?"

"Ew." Ken Roberts lowers his phone. "She's not coming up on Google."

"Look on Two-Ton Tutti's Insta," Ken Hilton says.

Ken Roberts and Ken Carson hover over a photo of Tommy on Ken Roberts's phone. They look from each other to Ken Hilton like he should be put on a 5150 psychiatric hold, and not just for the Young Hollywood glamour.

"Thomas is so thirsty she'd gladly drink our douche juice just to feel closer to us," Ken Hilton says. "That's what we need. An insecure blank canvas to coat with jiz, sparkles and vodka. The Kens' mind, body and soul!"

"She does look kind of familiar," Ken Roberts says.

Ken Hilton shrugs. "I think we've been in the same class since elementary."

"All basic people look the same to me."

"Dude." Ken Carson hits Ken Roberts's shoulder. "You are, like, so racist."

"Our STARmeter is going to plummet." Ken Roberts stares back down at Tommy's photo. "She's ratchet!"

Ken Hilton drops his comb into his Disney princess makeup bag that has "I Woke Up Like This" written across the bottom. The motion makes Ken Roberts wince, like he expects Ken Hilton to throw it at him.

"You're just not seeing her potential," Ken Hilton says. "We'll have to change everything about her, but once she's exactly like us she'll be perfect."

Ken Roberts and Ken Carson force a smile and bobble their heads in unison. They aren't thrilled about getting a new sister—they don't share anything except needles. But they know better than to question Ken Hilton when his mind is programmed.

"I don't know, bruh," Ken Carson tells Ken Roberts. "But we do need volunteer credits this semester."

HOMECOMING GAME

Ken Carson's jumbo-butt fills the Jumbotron.

A buzzer sounds for halftime and the Barks players run to the sidelines to down spiked Gatorade—what can it hurt? They're down twenty points. Their uniforms are pink and black. Formerly red and white, but Ken Hilton made Principal Elliot change them.

The Willows High cheer squad, led by Ken Roberts, does cartwheels onto the field. They're the opening act for Sandy Hooker.

According to his latest status update, Ken Hilton, a.k.a. Sandy Hooker, is saying a pre-show prayer (muttering "ohm" as a minion sprinkles pink glitter over him) in his private tent positioned at the end of the field.

Tommy sits with Tutti and Allan on the bleachers waiting for the game to start.

"I saw a comment on SoFamous claiming that for Sandy Hooker's encore she's going to scan the crowd and randomly pick someone to give a lap dance to," Tutti says. "Do you think it's true?"

"I heard she resurrected Alexander McQueen to get him

to design her costume," Tommy says. He grabs a handful of popcorn from the bag Tutti's holding and shoves the kernels in his mouth. The atmosphere on the bleachers is tense, like an Illuminati ritual is about to start.

Allan, wearing a graphic tee with an alien head that says "I Don't Believe in Humans," isn't at all interested in Ken Carson's majestic ass, Ken Roberts's split legs or Ken Hilton's latest stunt. Tommy wonders why he even came to the game. He's reading a book called *This Perfect Day*. It must've been ordered online. There's only one bookstore in Willows and it sells nothing but *Valley of the Dolls* and diet books.

Tommy spots Blaine on the stairs and waves him over. Allan finally looks up from his book.

"This is the weirdest football game I've ever been to," Blaine says as he reaches them. "I saw Coach Summers behind the tent wearing latex shorts and a dog collar. Interesting way to rouse team spirit . . ."

"No, no." Tommy shuffles over to make room. "He's one of Sandy Hooker's backup dancers!"

"Ah." Blaine nods. "Glad that's cleared up."

"It's not that far of a stretch if you've taken his sex ed class." Tutti shrugs.

Tommy introduces her and Allan to Blaine.

"You have the best eyebrow arch I've ever seen," Tutti tells him.

Allan rolls his eyes. And Sandy Hooker hasn't even started performing yet.

The cheerleaders finish their routine with Ken Roberts spinning through the air. There are other guys on the squad, but he's the only one who refuses to wear the male version of the uniform. He's wearing tight flesh-colored underwear beneath his skirt, which makes it look like he's not wearing any underwear at all, but creates an odd smoothness over his bulge.

Principal Elliot steps onto the stage holding a mic.

"Willows High welcomes you to the Crush Cream Soda homecoming game halftime show," he shouts in his best announcer voice. "Now presenting San-dy Hooker!"

The crowd screams like they're in a school shooting.

A rotating eight ball descends from the top of the stage and splits open to reveal Sandy Hooker. She's wearing a string of bullets around her fake boobs, thigh-high pink latex boots with at least fifty-inch heels, and a sequined miniskirt that is about to burst at the seams. Her tuck is lit.

Sandy Hooker doesn't do much—she lip-syncs about as well as Mariah Carey during *Dick Clark's New Year's Rockin' Eve*, and struts from one end of the stage to the other and back again, her ass implant slipping out from beneath the restraint of her sequins.

Tommy is mesmerized. Sandy Hooker is the most magnificent piece of trash he has ever seen.

"I feel like I need to be tested for gonorrhea," Allan says.

When Tommy looks over at Blaine to see his reaction, he feels a stab of jealousy. Blaine is staring at Ken Hilton like everyone stares at Ken Hilton. Like he's a rare solar eclipse you can't resist looking at, even if it's bad for you. He burns into your eyes, leaving you seeing white spots, he's so radiant. Everything you look at afterward pales in comparison. Tommy self-consciously touches the scar on his cheek.

"Hunty" ends with a series of on-stage explosions. Sandy Hooker is left in a swirl of fog, a single spotlight cast down upon the set of fake eyelashes over her already fake eyelashes. Coach Summers crawls off the stage, red marks on his skin from where Sandy Hooker whipped him.

Sandy Hooker basks in the glory of her applause. As Tommy watches, it's like she's getting bigger and bigger. "Drink Me" is written on the waistband of her underwear.

The encore starts, a slow, sultry beat. The faces of the crowd flash on the screen of the Jumbotron above the stage. Sandy Hooker blocks the spotlight with her hand as she pretends to scan the crowd. Tommy can tell she already knows what comes next. Ken Hilton is a master manipulator.

"Are you bitches in my gang?" Sandy Hooker yells into the mic. Rapturous applause. "You wish!" Sandy Hooker laughs. "And for one of you, your wish is my command . . ."

The camera slowly moves across the bleachers.

"I knew it!" Tutti exclaims. "I wonder who she's going to pick."

Tommy feels like there's something inside of him scratching to get out. Tutti places her hand on his knee as the image projected on the Jumbotron comes nearer to the spot where they're sitting.

"Why be you when you can be me?" Sandy Hooker purrs into the mic.

The crowd has gone quiet. No one knows if it's time for a sacrifice or a summoning.

The camera slowly moves through the crowd. It's only two bleachers away from Tommy now. He feels the thrashing in him intensify.

"Threesomes are so over," Sandy Hooker says. "Foursomes are everything now. Four is the magic number."

Tutti's grip on Tommy's leg tightens.

"Did she just say . . . a fourth?" she asks.

When the camera reaches their bleacher, Allan is the first to appear on the screen. He doesn't even notice. He has his nose back in *This Perfect Day*.

The camera moves over to Tutti. She steals a look at herself on the screen and flips her blue hair, blowing the crowd a kiss.

But the camera doesn't hold on her. It keeps moving. When it lands on Tommy, his chest constricts and he stares down at his feet, expecting the camera to quickly move on. But when he looks up, it's still frozen on his face. The people in the surrounding bleachers all turn from the Jumbotron to look directly at Tommy. The camera goes close-up on his face.

"I'd introduce myself," Sandy Hooker says from the stage, "but I don't speak Bark."

The crowd laughs. Tommy wants to bury his face in his hands, to get up and run, to disappear. But he still hasn't taken a breath.

Over the laughter, Sandy Hooker booms into the mic. "I'm going to kill you and bring you back to life a star!"

The crowd goes wild.

"Go get him, gurs," Sandy Hooker tells Ken Roberts and

Ken Carson, who hop across the field and up the stairs to where Tommy is sitting.

Tutti is practically jumping out of her seat. "I can't believe it!" she screams over the cheering crowd. "You're going to be a Ken!"

It all happens so fast. Ken Carson steps on Blaine's toes to pull Tommy to a stand. The next thing Tommy knows, Ken Carson is lifting him onto his shoulders. Ken Roberts shakes his pom-poms as he skips in front of Ken Carson and Tommy back down the stairs. They bring Tommy to the stage.

When Ken Carson puts him down, Tommy's knees buckle. He's standing so close to Sandy Hooker he can smell the vodka on her breath.

"The face will have to be permanently contoured and the nose reconstructed before we can make our final decision," Sandy Hooker says.

The crowd stops cheering and listens intently. Tommy realizes Sandy Hooker is talking about him.

"And while you're under we'll declaw you, give you cheek, ass and pec implants, new teeth, collagen in your lips and an arch on your left eyebrow so you can have permanent bih face too. It'll just take a little Botox, and then, of course, it'll be your responsibility to maintain. My father will suggest every three months, but he's just a greedy bastard. Once every six months should suffice."

Sandy Hooker pinches Tommy's cheek.

"Well, maybe every three for you. You have terrible elasticity!"

The crowd laughs. Sandy Hooker pans to them.

"But what do you think, Willows High? With the right packaging and a total rebrand, then maybe, um, what's your name?" Sandy Hooker shoves the mic in front of Tommy's mouth like they've never met.

"Tommy," Tommy says with a trembling voice. "Tommy Rawlins."

Sandy Hooker yanks the mic back.

"Then maybe Thomas could be marketable," he says. "Let me hear it, Willows High! Would you buy a new Ken?"

The crowd cheers louder than ever, chanting, "Ken, Ken, Ken!"

"The people have spoken," Sandy Hooker exclaims, turning back to Tommy with a wicked glimmer in her bloodshot eyes. "My father will see you at his clinic tomorrow morning. You're in good hands. He's rated the best plastic surgeon in the state."

Ken Roberts can't contain himself. He grabs Sandy Hooker's mic.

"And he doesn't have a license!" he squeals, sounding like Minnie Mouse after a crack binge.

Sandy Hooker looks like she might hit Ken Roberts with the mic.

"Did I click Send out of your mouth?" she asks.

The crowd "oohs." Ken Roberts blushes with embarrassment, but with all the stage lights he just looks slightly more fake-baked than usual.

"Once the bandages come off, we'll give you the blond tiara," Sandy Hooker tells Tommy. "And if the selfie you take after the makeover is complete gets Liked by everyone who's anyone at Willows High, we'll put you on display."

Sandy Hooker smiles at Tommy, a Matryoshka doll with a million equally deceiving smiles underneath.

"What do you think, Thomas?"

Sandy Hooker places the mic in front of Tommy's mouth and quickly pulls it away.

"That was a trick question. Duh, thinking is for people with wrinkles!"

Laughter from the stands.

Sandy Hooker chants, "Chin up! Shoulders back! Heels on! Don't look back!"

The crowd repeats after her, over and over, stomping their feet on the bleachers.

Tommy swallows a mouthful of creamy pink vomit.

"Don't look so scared." Sandy Hooker giggles. "It's just playtime."

DISCOUNT BIN

As the second half of the game starts, Tommy sneaks off with Allan by his side. Tommy's in an absolute daze. The people in the bleachers stop cheering and go quiet as he ducks past. Phones lift and Tommy is blinded by flashing cameras.

Allan is talking a mile a minute next to him, but Tommy just smiles. He can't stop smiling. It's like it's already painted on his face.

Tomorrow morning. Dr. Hilton will guide him into his light. From the light he came, and to the light he shall return! If you don't drift into the afterlife from anesthesia during a late-in-life plastic surgery procedure, then you'll never make *Willows Daily*'s obituaries section. They only run before-and-after photos.

Allan is listing the reasons why Tommy "cannot, under any circumstances, go through with this."

Tommy nods his head absently. He hasn't stopped trembling since his face appeared on the Jumbotron. When he stepped off the stage he almost fell flat onto the grass. His legs were like jelly. Allan and Tutti rushed down from the bleachers to reach him. The cheer squad all tried to take selfies with him at once. Tutti held them back while Tommy and Allan made a run for it. Blaine was lost in the crowd.

"Do you believe in the devil?" Tommy asks Allan, cutting him off mid-list. He's at number thirty: because what happens when a gaping hole goes out of style?

"You are not evil." Allan stops at his car. "Don't let Ken Hilton make you one of his dolls!"

"You don't think I can do it," Tommy says. "Is that it?"

"What? No!"

"You don't think that I can walk the walk, and talk that bitchy clipped-talk, and pout, and deep throat, and never eat again! You don't think I can be popular. You think that I'm destined to be a loser forever."

"No, Tommy, that's not it. I just never thought you were a loser to begin with."

"You're right, I'm not a loser. If I were a loser, if I weighed two tons like Tutti, or wore Urban Outfitters–reject graphic tees like you, then at least I'd be written about on SoFamous. At least then I'd exist!"

Allan opens his car door, then slams it closed again. Tommy's surprised it doesn't fall right off.

"Is this about that stupid site?" Allan asks. "You should be thankful that you've never been on it!"

"Yeah, right."

"I'm serious! Did you ever stop and think that the reason the Kens never put you on their Tumblr is because you're different?"

"Every day."

"And that they're jealous? The Kens are so insecure that they all have to be exactly the same to feel powerful. You don't need them, and that terrifies them."

Allan pushes his glasses up his nose.

"You're Tommy. Not Ken. You're . . . sweet. You cry every time you have to kill a prostitute in a video game to move ahead; you laugh out loud in physics class when the teacher talks about Kundt's tube . . ."

Tommy snickers.

"And you're the only person I can hang out with and even if we don't say a word it's comfortable. It's real."

Allan gets into his car.

"I don't want to lose that," he says as Tommy slides into the passenger seat next to him.

It takes a few tries but the car finally starts. Tommy doesn't know where his shaking and the car's rattling start and end.

"Do you really trust Ken Hilton?" Allan asks as he backs out of the parking lot. "Why the sudden interest in you?"

"We were close once."

"I know. And how'd that end?"

Tommy stares back at the field as they pull onto the street. He can see the Jumbotron in the distance. Ken Carson dashes across the field.

"Maybe he finally sees potential," Tommy says.

"Overnight? And why such a public display? Ken Hilton treats everything like a game."

"Don't you get it? I want to play!"

"Think about what you're saying. What it would mean! We're talking about changing everything about you."

"I know. Isn't it great? But I won't be able to recover from surgery at home. My parents will freak out."

Allan grips the steering wheel so hard his knuckles go white. "I should hope so!"

"No, I mean my mom will assume I'm doing it to get on a reality show, and she'll cry about how excited she is for me to have finally found a career I'm interested in. And my dad will live-tweet throughout my recovery. I cannot make them that happy. Please, Allan, can I crash at your place?"

"No way. I don't want any part in this!"

"I'll tell my parents we're doing SAT prep or something. Or, will you tell them for me?" Tommy gives Allan his best puppy-dog eyes. That look will be so much more successful when his eyes are the shape and color of a Ken's. But it does the trick on Allan as he glances over. It usually does.

"You want me to lie to your parents?"

"Well, I can't. What if my new nose grows?"

"And what exactly do you expect me to tell *my* parents?"

"They'll never know. I'll stay in the pool house. Your mom is a housewife of Willows Hills—they only ever go in there to bang the pool boy!"

Margaret and George Rawlins don't put up any resistance when Allan asks them, during dinner that night, if Tommy can stay over for a while. Tommy's almost offended by their lack of involvement in the conversation. They barely look up from their phones. His parents have always been more in tune with the Willows frequency than he is. Tommy feels like an outcast everywhere, even at home. This is his chance to finally connect.

Allan shrugs at Tommy across the table.

"It'll just be for a week," Tommy says. "We'll be doing SAT prep."

"Okay, son." His father cuts into his kale.

"Just put the dates you'll be away in the Google calendar, dear," is all his mother says. She's in a somber mood. She filed a missing person's report when she realized Roomsy had come out of the closet and disappeared. She'd long suspected her of being lesbian. If it weren't for the emotional support of Alexa, she'd be inconsolable.

"We won't stay up too late, I promise," Tommy says, desperate. "No wild parties . . ."

"Oh, you boys." His mother winks.

"What do you mean, 'you boys'?" Tommy asks.

"You don't have to lie to us. We're modern parents, Tommy. If you want to spend the week in The Hills with your lover we're not going to stand in your way."

"What are you talking about? Allan and I are just friends."

"You mean you aren't packing each other's fudge?" his dad asks.

"No!" Tommy almost falls out of his chair. "Allan isn't even gay. I mean, hello, look at what he's wearing! And his hair's messy! And he's never stepped foot in a gym. He's not even an ally. He doesn't even watch *RuPaul's Drag Race!*"

"You mean you're actually going to stay at Allan's house to study?" his mother asks, an even more wounded look on her face than the one on Allan's, who is staring down at his plate. Her lips become a thin line and she gets up from the table. "I'll get dessert," she says, forcing a smile. "We're having kale chips!"

Up in his room after dinner, Tommy sits on the edge of the bed trying to pack and mostly staring off at the glowing WILLOWSLAND sign through his window. A suitcase is open at his feet, but he's not bringing much—none of his clothes will fit over his new implants. He drops a roll of socks into the suitcase.

"Sorry about my parents thinking we're boyfriends," he tells Allan, leaning against the doorway.

"I wasn't offended."

Tommy zips up the suitcase and rolls it to the door.

"Okay," he says, hitting the light switch. "I'm ready."

The old model gets left behind.

PART 2

LIFE-SIZE

"I like to think of my life as an impossible dream."

RUTH HANDLER

THE FACTORY

Shiny happy people come out of Dr. Hilton's clinic. Taut, smooth skin. Stretched sin. Pointed tips, blown-up lips, American-youth tits. Tommy pretty-people watches over the pages of *People* magazine as he sits in the waiting room next to Tutti.

Allan had refused to take him to his appointment, so Tommy called Tutti. He knows this whole thing is crazy, but it's like contemplating infinity . . . he can't really grasp what he's about to do. The idea of being a Ken still seems so remote, just another one of his fantasies. He doesn't really believe it's about to happen. *It's just playtime.*

Ken Hilton started an Instagram account for him: @KenRawlins. It already has thousands of followers. Ken Hilton texted him the password: bihimken. Tommy's first post is going to be a post-surgery selfie. And it's going to make him a star.

"Why is Allan acting so mutilated?" Tommy asks Tutti.

"He just likes you the way you are," Tutti says. "But I totally get it. Not that I think you need plastic surgery, but the Kens are lit. Are we going to lose you as a friend once you're sitting at the center table?"

"'Zif! The Kens all have their niche. Ken Roberts has the cheerleaders, Ken Carson has the jocks, and I'll have the misfits! You, Allan and . . . Blaine."

They're interrupted by Dr. Hilton bursting out of his office. He wears a white lab coat and has thin, wispy blond hair standing up on his head.

"Ah, hello Tommy." He air-kisses him. "Ken has told me so much about you."

"He has?"

"Well, all I need to know, at least. Cut deep!"

Dr. Hilton's eyes land on Tutti.

"But first, you must introduce me to your friend."

"This is Tutti. She's just here for moral support."

"She's here because Baphomet sent her," Dr. Hilton says, pulling up a waiting-room chair and taking Tutti's hands in his own. "Young lady, the good Lord has sent you to me. It just so happens I'm looking for a pro-bono charity case, you know, for my image. So very hard to find in Willows. But I've been on the lookout. I want to see a headline saying I'm paying it forward."

"You want to give me money?" Tutti asks.

Dr. Hilton throws his head back with laughter. "No, you silly fat girl! I want to give you something much more valuable: a thin waist."

Tutti pulls her hands away.

"I was made this way," she says. "We have a responsibility to girls to reflect a broader view of beauty."

"Oh, I see." Dr. Hilton's forehead would totally be crinkled if it could move. "I didn't realize you were mentally ill. That's a little too philanthropic for my agenda." He turns to Tommy. "Do you have any other fat friends?"

Dr. Hilton doesn't wait for an answer. He claps his hands together and jumps to a stand.

"Come, Ken," he says, pulling Tommy into the surgery room. "That's what you're going to be doing every time you look in the mirror when I'm through with you!"

Tommy looks back at Tutti from the doorway.

"Good luck," she mouths.

The door closes and Dr. Hilton leads Tommy to a surgical chair surrounded by an anesthesiologist and nurses wearing pink face masks.

"So, what *exactly* are you going to do to me?" Tommy asks Dr. Hilton, who is snapping on his latex gloves.

"You have to do everything to *be* everything." The doctor motions to the anesthesiologist. "Now just lie back and relax," he says.

Tommy drifts off to Dr. Hilton singing, "A spoonful of propofol helps the ugly go down, the ugly go down, the ugly go down . . ."

STORAGE WAREHOUSE

The night after the surgery is spent at Dr. Hilton's clinic, and the next morning Tommy is released. Tutti picks him up in her Volkswagen Beetle and brings him to Allan's to recover.

"How do I look?" Tommy murmurs as Tutti leads him into the pool house.

"You look like a mummy," she says.

Tommy's whole body is bandaged. Tutti helps him into bed.

"Bring me a mirror," Tommy says.

Allan is standing in the corner of the room, horrified. He puts his hands in his pockets and then runs them through his hair, unsure of what to do with himself. Finally, he gets a bottle of water and a straw and brings it to Tommy's mouth.

"Drink. And don't try to talk. You need to rest."

"A mirror!" Tommy insists. He's lucid enough to know that he won't be able to see the changes yet, that he's swollen and bruised and covered in bandages. But he wants to look into his glazed, out-of-focus eyes to see if they've become slits.

Allan sighs and goes to the bathroom. He comes back out with a handheld mirror. Tommy tries to take it, but he can't lift his hand. Allan holds it up for him.

"It's *so* Joan Rivers," he jokes.

Tutti laughs, and so does Tommy, which is painful.

"The pills," he cries, giving up on his reflection. He can't keep his eyes open long enough to see himself.

"Sounding like a Ken already."

Tutti opens one of the several bottles of pain meds Dr. Hilton prescribed for Tommy. He went a little prescription happy. He's used to writing prescriptions by the dozen for his wife.

The drugs take effect swiftly. Tommy drifts into a sweet dream.

All week, Allan takes care of Tommy, skipping school for the first time in his life. Allan feeds him and even helps him to the bathroom. He keeps him stoned and pain free. Tommy sleeps most of the time, but Allan is right there every time he wakes up.

When he is conscious, Tommy begs Allan to help him remove the bandages—just for a peek. But Allan refuses.

"You have an appointment to have them removed next week," he says. "But it won't exactly be a revelation. You already know you're going to look like a Ken."

Tommy picks up his phone from his nightstand and logs

onto his Instagram account. He's gotten a thousand new followers since going in for surgery.

He takes a selfie of his bandaged head.

"Well," Allan says, "if you're well enough to take a selfie I guess that means I don't have to be your around-the-clock nurse anymore."

He picks up the remote and motions to the TV.

"I downloaded some of your favorite movies to keep you occupied while I'm at school. *Death Becomes Her, Bedazzled*— 1967 and 2000 versions—and, of course, *Clueless.*"

"Have I told you lately I love you?" Tommy risks the pain by stretching his face into a smile. Allan just stares at the TV.

Tommy wonders if Blaine is one of his followers, but when he searches for him he doesn't come up. Blaine is off the grid.

"Have you seen Blaine?" Tommy asks. "At school?"

"I haven't been at school," Allan says. "I've been taking care of you . . . But I did go in yesterday for a test. You were zonked out anyway. He was there. He asked how you're recovering."

"He did?" Tommy brings his hands to his bandaged cheeks.

"Yeah." Allan drops the remote next to Tommy. "Any other movies you want me to download?"

―――

"Look at the sky, Tommy," Allan says. It's the middle of the night and they're sitting out by the pool. Tommy's sleep patterns are wonky because of the painkillers. Allan's hyped up on coffee to get through studying for the classes he's been missing. "Do you see that?" he asks. "It's Sirius B!"

Tommy lifts his head and tries to focus his eyes, peering through the space in his bandages. "What am I supposed to be looking at?"

Allan turns off the pool lights so they can get a better view.

"It's one of eight known degenerate dwarfs in our solar system," he says. "It's very rare to be able to see it without a telescope."

"A degenerate dwarf? Did you take some of my meds?"

"Also known as a white dwarf. See it?"

Tommy's so fucked up he can barely see two inches in front of him.

"It's referred to as the 'Pup' star to Sirius's dog." Allan helps Tommy lean back in his pool lounger and lies beside him. They stare up at the sky. "It's the smaller star next to Sirius—the brightest star in our solar system," Allan explains. "It wasn't discovered until the '70s. It's usually whited out by Sirius's light."

Tommy's wobbly head lands on Allan's shoulder.

"'Sirius rises late in the dark, liquid sky,'" Allan says. "'On summer nights, star of stars / Orion's Dog they call it, brightest / Of all, but an evil portent, bringing heat / And fevers to suffering humanity.'"

"Did you just make that up?" Tommy asks.

"Homer, *The Iliad*."

"Are those elements? You know I'm failing biology, Allan."

Allan sighs, his cheek against Tommy's hair. Still brown. The last semblance of him. It's greasy. He hasn't been able to shower in his bandages. Allan doesn't mind.

"We learn the periodic table in chemistry. Oh, Tommy. Never change."

"You reek like tacos," Tommy says.

"Job hazard." Allan laughs. "The Pup star packs mass comparable to the Sun's into a volume that is significantly smaller than the Sun. That's what makes it so special. It might not be as bright and shiny as Sirius A, with its overpowering glow, but"—Allan glances down at Tommy, snoozing on his shoulder—"but it doesn't need to be as flashy to be as powerful," he whispers.

DIP-A-DEE-DOO-DAH

When the bandages are removed, Dr. Hilton shows no reaction. He takes a step back, staring at Tommy's freshly molded naked body.

Dr. Hilton stares for so long that Tommy starts to worry. Is something wrong? Shouldn't Dr. Hilton be foaming at the mouth? What if he's horribly disfigured from the surgery? Deformed Ken! He'll definitely be sent back to the manufacturer.

Tommy looks down at his own body, trying to see what's wrong. His chest is huge. And his abs. He has *eight* of them. Tommy's neck squeaks as he strains it to try to get a look at his new ass.

"Careful." Dr. Hilton gently turns his head forward. "Don't want to break you! You're a masterpiece."

Dr. Hilton gets a misty look in his eyes. A strand of his wispy hair sticks up and gently sways on the top of his head.

"Doctor, what's wrong?" Tommy picks up a scalpel to try to see his reflection. "Is something the matter with my face?" He's sure Dr. Hilton wasn't able to smooth out his scar, that he'll never be perfect.

The doctor's eyes grow so wide he looks absolutely crazed.

"No, my sweet boy! I just injected a little too much Dilaudid into my ankle this morning."

Tutti doesn't say anything when Tommy steps out of Dr. Hilton's office. She just stares up at him with her mouth gaping. If he gets this kind of reaction wearing pajama bottoms and a loose-fitted shirt, he can only image the reaction once he's all dolled up.

They walk out of the clinic to Tutti's Bug in silence. She puts the key in the ignition and turns to look at Tommy, then back out the front windshield, then back at him, struggling to find the right words. They drive down the street.

"How do you feel?" she finally asks.

"Sore," Tommy says. "And a bit awkward. I'm not used to moving in this body. I feel like my skin is a costume."

Tommy lowers the passenger-seat visor and looks at his reflection in the mirror. The scar on his cheek is barely visible thanks to all of the filler. It's like Dr. Hilton took sandpaper to his skin. He's so smooth! Every inch of him looks like a poster of a real thing on a wall in a bedroom of a house in another house and so on and so on for all of eternity.

"You look *just* like *them*," Tutti says with wonder in her voice.

"I can't wait to show Allan!" Tommy says. "Is he at home?"

"Working. Want to stop for a taco?"

"No." Tommy traces his tongue over his sparkling white veneers. "I want to go back to the pool house and look in the full-length mirror!"

Tutti squeezes his bicep implant as they stop at a red light.

"It's so eerie," she says. "The only thing that's missing is the hair. I can bleach it for you, if you want. I have the perfect toner. Remember when I was blonde? You even said you were jealous because it was exactly the Kens' shade."

"Yes!" Tommy exclaims. "I can't exactly afford to go to Ken Hilton's salon. I may have the Kens' face, but I don't have their wallet. At least not yet. Ken Hilton has been such a fairy godmother, I wouldn't be surprised if he somehow found a way to make me rich. Can there be a poor Ken?"

"You don't need money." Tutti laughs. "Kens get everything for free. Usually people give it to them willingly, but if they don't, the Kens just take it. No one would dare put a Ken in cuffs. Unless they were pink and fluffy and a Ken absolutely begged them to."

Tommy's life is never going to be the same!

"Just remember, if Ken Hilton is your fairy godmother, that means he can take everything away as quickly as he gave it."

"The clock doesn't strike twelve in Ken World," Tommy says. "It's always eleven eleven."

Tutti stops at her house to pick up the dye, and then they go back to Allan's pool house for the treatment. Tommy imagines that the bleach burning his scalp is seeping into his brain, matching his interior with his exterior, whiting out his fears and feelings and pesky morals . . .

"All you need is some gel," Tutti says after rinsing his hair in the sink. She digs through the bathroom drawers but comes up empty. "Do you think Allan has any in his room?"

"Are you kidding? He doesn't even comb that ginge."

"I'll run to the drugstore," Tutti says. "You're not complete without it!"

"Dippity-Do," Tommy calls after her.

"Of course!" she yells back.

Tommy almost tells Tutti to pick up a pair of blue contacts while she's out, but the Kens have their contacts specially made. Perfectly Possessed™.

PILL BOMB

Until the swelling goes down and he's ready to make his debut as a Ken, Tommy stays locked up in the pool house. He practices posing for selfies from every angle, searching the pool house for the best light, but he doesn't post any of them. There's only one chance to post like a Ken, and like everything else from this point forward in Tommy's life, it has to be flawless.

When Allan saw Tommy's unbandaged face for the first time he made no expression. He didn't utter a peep. But Tommy has caught him stealing little glances ever since.

A few days after Tommy's bandages are removed, Allan gets home from a shift at Taco Accessory. He flops down on the couch in his uniform.

"I brought you a burrito," he says, turning on the TV.

"I can't get cellulite on my new ass!" Tommy blocks the screen with his twerking butt. "What do you think?" he asks.

"It's so *big*." Allan laughs. He can't look away. Tommy starts laughing too, so hard he falls over and doesn't even feel it; his ass implants protect him. He just sort of bounces a little, which makes him laugh even harder.

He gets off the floor and sits on the couch next to Allan.

"I have to make sure the first selfie I post is on point," he says, scrolling through the photos he's taken of himself. "You heard what Ken Hilton said: if his court doesn't approve, I won't be made a Ken."

"Yeah, and if you miss any more classes you won't be a made a graduate. You really want to flunk junior year?"

"The Kens always get a 100 emoji."

"I bring assignments home for you and they just sit in a pile while you stain the pool house mirrors with your jiz. Have you even looked at the math sheet I brought today?"

"Math class is tough."

"I'm not doing it for you," Allan says.

Tommy gives him puppy-dog eyes.

"No way." Allan jumps up from the couch. "I'm not a Ken's bitch."

"Please, Allan," Tommy begs. "I have so much to do. I need to pick a filter!"

There's a knock on the pool house door.

"Tell your mother to have her affair at *his* house," Tommy tells Allan as he goes to open it.

Allan gives him a look. "Not every housewife who lives in The Hills is like Ken Hilton's mother, Tommy." He opens the door. "What are *you* doing here?" he asks.

When Blaine steps inside, Tommy's heart starts beating

so hard he almost expects his left pec implant to pop out.

"Blaine." He flutters his new eyelashes. "What a surprise."

"I wanted a sneak preview," Blaine says. "The whole school is talking about you."

Tommy covers his face with his hands. "I probably look terrifying! I'm not wearing any foundation, and I'm still all swollen."

"Let me see." Blaine pulls Tommy's hands away. Tommy doesn't really resist. He's not that swollen anymore, and Ken-skin looks permanently airbrushed anyway. "So is this what you were asking for in the cemetery?" Blaine asks.

They hold eye contact and Tommy feels a shiver run up his spine.

"When did you meet in the cemetery?" Allan says behind them.

Blaine points at items on the coffee table.

"What's all this?" he asks. There are plastic bowls and spoons, a measuring scale, a safety fuse, a drill, one of Tommy's empty pill bottles, a bottle of potassium perchlorate and aluminum powder.

"Allan's making a pill-bottle bomb with one of my bottles of meds," Tommy says. "Dr. Hilton kind of over-prescribed."

"A bomb?" Blaine looks at Allan with a newfound appreciation.

"For his channel," Tommy explains.

"How does it work?" Blaine asks.

"Simple." Allan picks up the empty pill bottle. "You drill a hole through the cap for the fuse, then cut a good length of safety fuse and stick it through the hole, tying one end to secure it. Measure the chemicals, and then—"

"Half and half?" Blaine interrupts.

"No." Allan shakes his head. "Two parts potassium perchlorate, one part aluminum powder. Then you fill the bottle one-third full with the powder. You want to detonate in an open field, obviously."

"Obviously," Blaine says.

SHOP TILL YOU DROP

The first photo Tommy posts as @KenRawlins blows up. He watches as the hundreds of Likers turn to thousands.

Tommy shows Allan the number as they lounge by the pool. Allan is prone to sunburn, and his nose is completely white with sunscreen. He's so pale compared to Tommy, who looks like the sun did a lot more than just kiss him.

A new comment pops up on his post every second. Mostly, everyone's voicing approval over his remodel.

"Someone called me the Ken hotter than Ken Hilton!"

Tommy stops scrolling when the comments turn trolling.

"They're not living for my outfit, though," he says. "#basic."

"Hey, isn't that one of my shirts?" Allan asks.

Tommy looks down at the graphic tee he's wearing. It says, "You may not like me, but Jesus thinks I'm to die for."

"Exactly." He laughs.

As a Ken, Tommy will be expected to sit front row.

"What am I going to do, Allan? I don't have the money for a new wardrobe!" He takes another selfie and looks down at it disdainfully. "Screw it, I'll just steal. Why not? It's a win-win. If I don't get caught, I'll have new clothes. If I do get caught, I'll have a criminal record. Either way, I'm sure to officially be made a Ken."

"Oh, come on! I'll lend you my credit card."

"Are you offering to be my sugar daddy?"

Allan chokes. "You really are a Ken now."

Once Tommy gets the idea in his head, he's determined. It's the first time he's seriously contemplated stealing. Tommy Rawlins could never steal—but maybe Ken Rawlins can. It's the only way to find out if the transformation is complete.

Tommy is dying to know if he's dead inside.

Allan begrudgingly takes Tommy along with him to Willows Mall for his next shift at Taco Accessory. Tommy goes directly to the designer department store, which features heavily on the Kens' Instas. The sales associate doesn't look up from his phone as Tommy enters.

Tommy swallowed a handful of pain medication before leaving the pool house, so he's feeling chill. He pretends he really is a Ken and shops like it's his divine right. Rule number one: never look at price tags. Tommy just grabs whatever catches his eye. He moves fast, making his way around the store. He picks up a Hermès belt like a magic wand and simply summons.

He's about to be especially bold and ask the retail queen, who's currently on his phone, for a dressing room, but decides it's safer to sneak off unseen.

There are pliers in his backpack. Tommy came prepared, grabbing them from Allan's science supplies before they left the pool house. He quickly snaps off all the electronic tags on the clothes, which he then shoves in his bag with shaking hands. So the transformation *isn't* complete. A Ken's hands would never shake from nerves! Withdrawal maybe, but not nerves.

Tommy pokes his head out of the dressing room. The sales associate is busy FaceTiming, so Tommy casually walks out of the dressing room, coming to an abrupt stop when he sees *them*.

Alexander McQueen black leather boots with three buckles. The same ones Ken Hilton put on his wish list for one of his many admirers to buy. (Ken Hilton shops, but he never buys anything—he just takes photos of what he wants and posts them as demands.) Tommy can't believe his luck. The boots are in his size! Just imagine how jealous Ken Hilton will be.

His bag is stuffed, so Tommy slips off his old sneakers and puts them in the shoebox, unabashedly slipping the new boots on his feet.

Chin up! Shoulders back! Heels on! Don't look back!

Tommy walks straight out of the store.

He isn't expecting it when the alarm goes off. The boots! There must've been a security tag tucked inside.

"Excuse me, sir." A security guard approaches him. "Do you mind if I have a look in your bag?"

Tommy is terrified. All those sedatives he took are no match for the adrenaline shooting through his body. He fearfully meets the security guard's eyes, and realizes something's different. Tommy has never been looked at this way before. It's the look of a million fingers simultaneously swiping right on a dating app. So *this* is what it feels like to be devoured.

"Is there a problem?" Tommy asks, using a breathy voice he tried out in front of the mirror in Allan's pool house. He may just have to get out of this Ken style: on his knees. He's about to lure the security guard into the office, but then remembers a past scandal at Willows High when Ken Hilton leaked his underage sex tape on SoFamous. The post got so much attention that the Willows Police Department came to school to talk to Ken Hilton about the footage, which by then had been wiped off the net. No one had actually seen it. But *everyone* had commented on it.

Ken Hilton live-tweeted through his WPD interrogation. He even took a selfie with one of the police officers—Officer Simpson, as he later became known—posting it with the caption "pig play."

Everyone was shocked that Ken Hilton would even joke about having sex with someone who makes less than six figures a year. The comments on SoFamous were full of calls for his abdication. He explained himself in a blog post, saying that while it was okay to exploit the uniformed peasants, no self-respecting queen would ever actually sleep with one.

Tommy knows that he'll never be a Ken if he debases himself for a *security guard*. Only debase yourself for millionaires. That's, like, the law of the universe. Tommy thinks fast. WWKD?

It's like Ken Hilton is whispering in Tommy's ear: *Taser the bih.*

Tommy sees the Taser in the security guard's belt loop. He's thinking fast. He'll lead him to the office . . . get him on his knees . . . make him think he's going to . . . then he'll . . . and run out of the store, never looking back!

Kens only look back at the end of the year, when Facebook shows them their year in review.

Just then, Tommy hears a loud, shrill squeal.

The sales associate finally looks up from his phone, but he doesn't lower it. "Oh. My. Baphomet." He rushes up to Tommy and takes his photo. "You're the New Edition, aren't you?"

He excitedly poses next to Tommy for a selfie, then points at the security guard. "Is he bothering you?"

"Umm . . ." Tommy hesitates.

"You even *talk* like a Ken!" The sales associate wraps his arm around Tommy's shoulders and leads him out of the store. The alarm goes off but he ignores it, and the security guard is too busy staring at Tommy's ass to do anything. "Tell Ken Hilton I, like, *worship* Sandy Hooker," the sales associate says, waving enthusiastically as Tommy walks off. "And come back any time," he calls after him. "Kens get a 66.6 percent discount on everything!"

There's a line-up at Taco Accessory when Tommy walks into the food court, so he decides to use the bathroom to try on some of his clothes.

When he strips off Allan's graphic tee, Tommy brings it

up to his nose and smells it. Maybe not the most stylish wardrobe, but Tommy liked wearing Allan's clothes. They smell like Allan—comforting. Like fast-food grease and lab chemicals.

Tommy puts on a pink shirt and skinny jeans, stomping around the handicap bathroom in his McQueen boots.

When Tommy looks in the mirror, there's something different about his reflection. Well, everything's different. But something else. He doesn't know if it's from the severity of his blond hair, or the sharp point of his reconstructed nose, or the fact that he's now a criminal—but there is a corrupted twist to Tommy's face. His eyebrows are arched, and not just from the Botox, and his lips are permanently pursed with a glamorous superiority. Like he's just rubbed cocaine along the inside of his gums and is about to sell everyone's secrets to Radar Online.

Tommy struts straight out of the bathroom. Allan spots him from across the food court. He's in the middle of squirting sour cream onto a customer's burrito. He squeezes so hard when he sees Tommy, walking as if in slow motion toward him, that the cap of the bottle pops off and sour cream explodes everywhere. He has to roll an entirely new burrito. He's not the only one who's distracted. Tommy loses count of how many people look at him as he walks past. The Kens only count zeros anyway.

"So?" Tommy asks Allan once the Taco Accessory counter is clear. He does a little spin. "What do you think?"

"Well," Allan says. "You've sure mastered the look."

"You like?"

Allan stares at Tommy, trying to decide how to answer.

"Just do me a favor," he says. "Don't wear the Kens' contacts. Your eyes . . . they're the last part of you. I don't want to lose that."

Tommy's phone vibrates in the pocket of his bag. He pulls it out and reads a text message.

"Kiki at my place" is all it says.

WALL OF MIRRORS

The gate to Ken Hilton's Beaux-Arts mansion opens automatically as Tommy approaches. He walks up the driveway through fog lifting off the verdant grounds. A demonic gold-leaf doorknocker stares menacingly as he approaches the entrance.

Tommy can't believe he's back. He hasn't seen the Hilton house since he was seven years old, and it seems smaller than he remembers. He'd built it up in his memory as a palace, and with its French stone and marble pillars it isn't far off, but it's not exactly floating in the air.

Ken Hilton on the other hand . . . The maid opens the door and Ken Hilton descends the stairwell behind her looking like a GIF of a primetime soap opera from the '80s.

"It's *everything*," Ken Hilton says, walking straight up to him and poking his filler with his finger. "You're almost as pretty as me." Ken Hilton notices the McQueen boots on Tommy's feet and narrows his eyes. "*Suh k'yut*. Thanks for breaking them in for me, bih."

He takes Tommy up to his bedroom, which looks like it was designed by William Haines: Hollywood Regency furniture, sweeping drapes, everything glass and gilt. Ken Roberts and Ken Carson are positioned on his bed like dolls Ken Hilton sleeps with. The walls are all mirrored. Above the dresser hangs a giant framed portrait of Ken Hilton made out of thousands of tiny photos of Ken Hilton.

"Dude, do I know you from somewhere?" Ken Carson grins at Tommy. "You look, like, so familiar."

"I have one of those faces." Tommy smirks.

Ken Hilton has ten teacup dogs (all wearing diamond collars that weigh more than they do). They rush up to Tommy's legs as he enters the room, falling onto their side every time they bark.

"The blond is so much better than the brunette," Ken Roberts says. His bulimia breakfast breath wafts through the air.

"Totally," Ken Carson agrees, flexing his bronzed bicep. "Brunettes always look homeless."

"Does it suit me?" Tommy asks, self-consciously touching his scalp and looking into one of the walls. He winces—his scalp still burns from the bleach.

"The grass is always blonder on the other side," Ken Roberts says.

"Totally." Ken Carson finally drops his arm. "Look at the Lannisters, bruh. If incest is what it takes to keep them natural blonds, so be it."

Ken Hilton sits on the edge of his bed and his little dogs all try to jump on his lap at once. "These are my babies." Ken Hilton introduces them to Tommy. "This is Queen Ken Hilton, Princess Ken Hilton, Duchess Ken Hilton, Marchioness Ken

Hilton, Countess Ken Hilton, Viscountess Ken Hilton, Baroness Ken Hilton, Lady Ken Hilton, the Honorable Ken Hilton and Dame Ken Hilton, who doesn't get to sit on the bed because she's not a purebred!" Ken Hilton pushes the offending pup off his mattress. "Come," he tells Tommy, patting the spot on the bed next to him like Tommy's his newest pet.

They spend the rest of the day on Ken Hilton's bed reading about celebrities. There's little interaction, except the silent passing of lip gloss and the occasional smack of gushy pink lips.

After a while, Tommy gets restless and lifts his head from the blog he's reading off his phone. He can't help but be disappointed. He's finally hanging out with the Kens, and the expectation was high. If he's going to spend all day on Ken Hilton's bed, he at least hoped the rumors of the satanic orgies were true.

Ken Hilton closes his magazine and makes Tommy stand up so he can give him another look-over. He pinches his body, looking for fat.

"You've *almost* perfected the look," he says. "With a few minor adjustments you'll be ready for full display."

This is it! Tommy is finally being put on a shelf next to the Kens.

"Your selfie went viral," Ken Hilton says. "The peasants are so obsessed with my latest creation."

Ken Hilton turns to Ken Roberts and Ken Carson.

"What do you say, gurs?" he asks. "Is Thomas ready for his initiation?"

"He got Liked by the football team." Ken Carson shrugs.

"And the cheer squad," Ken Roberts adds. He drops his phone onto the bed with a dramatic sigh, turning to Tommy. "Make it good. I'm so bored. Leo's been with the same model, like, all week."

"I thought my selfie was the initiation?" Tommy asks.

"'Zif." Ken Hilton looks at him incredulously. "Right now you're just a thot with a bleach-out. You have to prove you're made of our material."

Tommy clutches his stomach full of nerves.

"Spill the tea." Ken Hilton passes Tommy his pink-rhinestone-encased iPhone.

Before Tommy can grasp it, Ken Hilton yanks his hand away.

"Do you know what this is?"

"Your phone?"

"Yes, but do you know whose phone it was before it was mine?"

"You have a used phone?" Tommy asks, not because he's a tech snob but because he's surprised. The only secondhand Ken Hilton is usually interested in is around his dick.

"This phone is sacred," Ken Hilton says. "It used to belong to Paris."

"You have Paris Hilton's old phone?"

"Don't ask how it came into my possession. I can't risk it getting out. Let's just say it involves the Bling Ring and an eight ball."

"I always thought you called yourself Ken Hilton because you're elite," Tommy says. "Do you really still care about Paris Hilton? It's not 2004."

Ken Roberts's cheek implants spread into a smile. "And here I thought you didn't have enough bitchiness in you to join the fam!"

"But be careful, newbie," Ken Carson warns. "Ken Hilton likes Heiress so much he uses it as a dildo, so unless you want him to break his bottle and use it as a dildo on you, it's probably best not to insult, like, the Hilton dynasty in his presence."

"And that includes the Richards sisters, bitch," Ken Hilton adds, dangling Paris Hilton's glimmering pink iPhone in front of Tommy's face. "So what do you say, Thomas? Are you ready to hold the Holy Grail?"

Tommy takes the phone with trembling hands.

"The initiation is a blog post on our Tumblr," Ken Hilton says. "If it's juicy enough, you can start posting on SoFamous regularly, using your Ken Rawlins account. For now, you can access through my phone. The password is 5150."

"What should I post?"

"A sex tape always says, like, 'I've arrived,'" Ken Carson suggests.

"You must have something on someone," Ken Roberts says. "What secrets have your friends told you?"

"I don't have a lot of friends."

Ken Roberts takes a selfie. "*Care* is only a word because it's in *scare*."

"Why am I here?" Tommy asks, only realizing he has spoken aloud when the Kens turn their heads in unison to look at him. "I mean, why am I the New Edition?"

Ken Roberts and Ken Carson lower their eyes.

Ken Hilton just keeps smiling. He picks up Dame Ken Hilton and kisses her wet, pink nose.

"Because even a mutt deserves a chance at life," he says.

The dog is dropped to the floor. It lands on its crooked tiara and yelps before scurrying away.

"But you're acting like . . . we didn't know each other before."

"You don't have a past," Ken Hilton says. "You're fresh out of the box." His eyes widen. "I know! Why don't you write a post about that geek you're always with? The one with that gay disease."

"You mean Allan Sherwood?" Tommy asks.

"Yeah, that freak. Do you have anything on him?"

"Wait," Ken Roberts says. "Allan Sherwood has HIV?"

"What are you talking about?" Ken Hilton glares.

"You just said 'the one with that gay disease.'"

"I meant gay as in lame. You are, like, so homophobic. HIV is not a gay disease, Ken Roberts. It's a poor person's disease."

"Allan has a disease?" Tommy asks.

"Duh." Ken Hilton rolls his eyes. "The ginger gene."

"Allan's my friend—"

"He's a fire-crotch with a two-figure allowance." Ken Hilton cuts Tommy off. "You're lucky we rescued you from his impoverished inferno of loser. He works in a food court, for Baphomet's sake!"

"Yeah, but Allan's not poor. He actually lives in The Hills. He only drives that old car because he refuses to accept his parents' money. He has integrity, or something."

"Ew." Ken Hilton reaches over and grabs his phone. "Let me see if there's anything we can use in your phone," he tells Tommy. "You're obviously not ready for the zenith."

Tommy passes Ken Hilton his phone, watching anxiously as Ken Hilton scrolls through it. He wracks his brain trying to think of what Ken Hilton is seeing, mostly just hundreds of practice selfies, and maybe some photos of him and Tutti and Allan . . . What kind of dirt is Ken Hilton expecting to find? But he obviously finds something. Tommy sees his blue eyes dilate with devilment. Ken Hilton shows Tommy and the Kens a photo of Tutti at her birthday party a few months earlier.

"Ken, you have a fan." Ken Hilton laughs at Ken Carson.

"Dude, is that supposed to be me?"

In the photo, Tutti is holding an Earring Magic Ken doll dressed in Ken Carson's number 69 football jersey.

"It was a joke," Tommy explains. "I made it for her birthday. You're her favorite."

"I am?" Ken Carson's smile is big and genuine. The Kens' resting bitch face is a smile, so Tommy can really tell the difference when it's real. For a glitch of the screen, Ken Carson almost looks human.

"You've made it when you've been molded in miniature plastic," Ken Hilton says. "But you know what children do with Barbie dolls . . . it's a bit scary."

Tommy gulps.

Ken Hilton's eyes twinkle.

"It practically writes itself," he says. "Text Tutti, Ken. Pretend you're, like, wet for her."

"Aw, bruh." Ken Carson moans. "What'd Tutti ever do to us?"

"Do you need to be rewired?" Ken Hilton asks.

Ken Roberts snickers. He loves when Ken Carson is in Ken Hilton's line of fire.

"There has to be something else that can be in my initiation post," Tommy says desperately.

"You should be grateful that I'm making Ken Carson do all the work," Ken Hilton says, throwing Tommy's phone back at him. "But it'll still count as your initiation. Everyone loves a good Two-Ton Tutti post. Of course, if you're going to eat lunch with us on Monday we have to do something about your eyes. Every time someone with brown eyes looks at me I feel like I'm about to be blown up."

"Fosh," Ken Roberts bobbles.

Ken Hilton opens his nightstand drawer and pulls out a package of contacts. He grabs Tommy by the wrist, dragging him over to one of the mirrored walls. Tommy isn't prepared for Ken Hilton's fingers jamming into his eyes.

The contacts are like two moons, pulling the tide within Tommy. He feels the flood pool into his pineal gland and drown the last semblance of his soul.

Tommy is still trying to blink his vision into focus when Ken Hilton unceremoniously jabs a diamond stud straight through his ear. Tommy screams out in pain.

"Remember who made you," Ken Hilton says.

FAMOUS FAMILY

After the Ken tryouts, Tommy goes home for the first time since his transition. He's exhausted. The Kens hazed him hard. The cracker they took turns jizzing on and made him eat contained *gluten*.

The walk from Ken Hilton's house down to the Mainland is even more depressing with the McQueen boots on his feet. Each step is a jingling struggle. Tommy's pierced ear bled onto the boots, so Ken Hilton told him to keep them.

At first, Tommy's parents are too distracted by the trending topics to notice the changes in their son. They sit down for dinner, and Siri says grace.

God is good.

God is great.

Let us thank him for our food.

And our followers.

When his mom finally does look at Tommy, her mouth drops open. She stares at him like he's a picture on a magazine in a news stand, wincing, as if recalling the birthing pain paper cuts of having delivered such a trashy tabloid cover.

His dad blinks and takes off his glasses, squinting at

Tommy. He lifts his phone and takes a picture. When the changes on Tommy's face appear on the screen, he knows they're real.

"Is getting plastic surgery a part of the SATs?" his father asks.

His mother starts crying. "You've been totally reconstructed. You have no idea how proud I am of you. I'll tag you in the Facebook post!"

* * *

The next morning is Sunday, and Tommy's parents take him to Famous Family Church to praise God for the "miracle."

Outside the church there is a statue of Jesus, Mary, Joseph and the three wise men (the only three in Willows) posing for paparazzi. Inside, the stained-glass windows depict the crucifixion. Instead of INRI written above the cross, it says GUCCI. The Madonna is literally Madonna wearing a Blond Ambition–era cone bra. Jesus is definitely on steroids, and is rocking a man bun.

As Tommy and his parents enter, something is off. Tommy usually feels so uplifted at church, partly from the GHB in the blood of Christ. But this morning, Tommy feels a deep foreboding. When he crosses himself with holy water, he almost expects it to burn . . .

But it just rolls off his artificial skin.

GIRLS' ROOM

Monday morning, Tommy gets picked up for school by Ken Hilton driving his pink Corvette. It honks in the driveway.

"Giddy up, bih!" Ken Hilton yells out the side of the convertible.

Tommy's mom peeks out the window, sipping her morning Keurig as Tommy puts on his boots.

"I just knew you'd make friends if you got a nose job." She smiles.

The Corvette honks again and Tommy comes flying out of the house. He knows better than to keep Ken Hilton waiting.

When he reaches the car, he realizes Ken Roberts and Ken Carson have been demoted to the backseat. They're both glaring at him. Tommy rides shotgun, and it feels like a throne.

Ken Hilton greets him by reading his outfit. Shredded skinny jeans and a deep-V-necked T-shirt. "Suburbia's sprawling." Ken Hilton laughs. Ken Hilton tells Tommy he's going to have to teach him everything, including the proper way to steal. Apparently jewelry is okay, but everything else makes him a klepto. Something about the difference between Lindsay and Winona . . .

"I can't believe you live in the ghetto," Ken Roberts says as they pass a three-story home with a Lexus in the driveway.

"Dude," Ken Carson says. "I thought you dropped off the face of the earth if you leave The Hills."

"You do," Ken Hilton says, turning his head and giving Tommy a half-smile. "But don't worry, Ken Roberts will help you find a sugar daddy and you'll have your own condo in The Hills in a jiffy!"

"If I can find one willing, that is." Ken Roberts fake-smiles in the backseat.

Ken Hilton pulls out a blunt from the glove compartment and sparks it. Tommy coughs as he takes a puff. His eyes turn even more bloodshot. They're already bothered by the contacts. He took them out before he went to bed, and all night he was tossing and turning, feeling so anxious about his first day at Willows High as a Ken.

He woke up nervous but felt fine after he got ready for school, especially once the contacts were in his eyes—he was synced.

The Corvette pulls up to the front of school and Tommy steps out, lit as fuck. One of Ken Hilton's minions parks his car for him.

When the doors of Willows High open, it's like the pandemonium of a store opening on Black Friday. Everyone wants the new merchandise.

Tommy looks through the crowd with total confidence. He isn't exactly sure where it's coming from, maybe the Ken wavelength from standing in a row with the other Kens. They move as one down the hallway. Legs extended in a straight line, it's a robotized strut, float, bounce. Tommy feels like he's on a runway.

The envy in everyone's eyes as they walk past elevates him. They don't see Tommy Rawlins. Like Ken Hilton really did create him. Tommy never was.

Allan and Tutti are standing at the lockers. He notices Ken Carson and Tutti share a look, but Tommy ghosts them. No, *Ken* ghosts them. Tommy could never be so transparently rude, but with the blue contacts in, his eyes only look directly at diamonds.

All of a sudden, Tommy loses his footing. His vision blurs, his heart starts racing and his stomach is in knots. He's so dizzy he has to lean on a locker to catch his breath. That's it, no more kush with his Lucky Charms!

The Kens keep walking. Allan and Tutti come up to Tommy.

"You okay?" Allan asks.

Tommy tries to even his breathing. What's happening? A second ago he was so confident, and now he's wracked with insecurity. "How am I doing?" he asks.

"I'd say fake it till you make it," Allan says. "But I guess in this case faking it is making it?"

Tommy laughs. "I miss you."

Allan blushes.

"Is the one-brown-one-blue your Ken look?" Tutti asks. "Or are you missing a contact?"

"Shit." Tommy surveys the floor. "I'm already messing up!"

"There it is." Allan spots the contact on the floor. Tommy

bends over to pick it up. Some Barks players at the end of the hall whistle at him. Tommy doesn't realize it's for him until he sees Allan's face turning even redder.

Ken Hilton sighs impatiently at the doorway of the girls' room. "We have to touch up before first period!"

"I better go rinse this off," Tommy says. "I'll catch you guys later, okay?"

"Pop off a leg." Tutti winks.

The Kens profess themselves to be "timeless," but if time does exist in their world, it's surely sped up. Minutes pass like the rotation of a disco ball. Tommy's head feels like it's spinning around his body.

"So, Ken Hilton," Ken Carson says as the Kens line up in front of the bathroom mirrors. Tommy takes the far sink. "Aren't you going to tell us about your date with your bae last night?"

Ken Hilton breathes so hard his hair actually moves. "There's nothing to tell. He had coke dick again!"

"Brad Curtis can't get it up?" Tommy asks. He rinses off his contact and puts it back in his eye. It's like swallowing a Xanax. Like swallowing a bottle of them. He's instantly calm. Tommy wipes a bead of sweat off his forehead. The bitch is back.

"A part of me wants to write all about it on SoFamous," Ken Hilton says, "but we're a shoo-in for prom king and queen, so I can't ruin his life until I'm wearing the crown."

"#rulestoliveby," Ken Roberts bobbles.

"Besides," Ken Hilton says, "it wouldn't just humiliate him, it would totally ruin me. If people know that Brad can't get it up, they'd know he just can't get it up for me. How many posts have we written on SoFamous about Francie Fairchild skipping class to abort his baby? He obviously has no problem getting it up for her."

"Brad broke up with Francie for you," Tommy says. He followed it obsessively. "You're the one he wants. He chose you over her, and she's the most popular girl in school!"

"Yeah, dude," Ken Carson says. "She has a double-jointed tongue."

Ken Hilton breaks down in fake sobs. "After the eight ball, Brad got confessional and told me they're still sleeping together! He's trying so hard to be gay for me, but he can only get turned on by girls. I even tried dressing up in drag!"

"Why don't you top him, dude?" Ken Carson suggests.

"I'm not doing all that work! I just want to lie there and then be given a piece of jewelry when it's over, like a lady."

Ken Hilton sprays himself with Heiress.

"But Brad's limp dick cannot leak." He gives Tommy and the Kens a warning look. "And I don't just mean literally. I mean, this can't get out to anyone. He'll never forgive me."

"Don't worry," Ken Roberts says, typing rapidly on his phone. "I can't keep a secret and my thoughts are tweets, but I started a private Twitter account for this exact reason. Your secret is secure with me."

"Thank Baphomet we're going to Dreamhouse tonight,"

Ken Hilton says, touching up his foundation. "I read on the event page that some frat boys are bringing their pledges to stick it in a dude, like a rite of passage."

Ken Carson smirks. "God bless academia, bruh."

The bell rings for class.

"We have gay history first period, so rearrange your schedule," Ken Hilton tells Tommy. "For today, we'll just meet up with you in the caf at lunch." Ken Hilton blows him a kiss before turning on his heels. "Don't be late, bih."

ON DOOMSDAY WE WEAR PINK

"So the new Ken is complete?" Brad Curtis gives Tommy a once-over as he sits next to Ken Hilton at the center table in the cafeteria.

The seat next to Ken Hilton is usually where Ken Roberts is placed, but he's shoved over to make room for the new product line. Ken Carson is across from them, looking all around the caf.

"I don't know, Ken, he may be even shinier than you." Brad winks at Tommy.

"He is shiny, isn't he?"

Ken Hilton brushes Tommy's hair back with his hand.

"He ought to be. My dad said his surgeries took twice as long as the other Kens . . ."

Tommy's eyes sting. He rubs his contacts, but it only makes the itching worse.

"Pre-game at my place before Dreamhouse tonight?" Ken Hilton asks.

"About that," Tommy says. "I don't think I can go. I don't have a fake I.D."

"Duh, we're underage twinks! Doors will open like wallets."

"Oh, well, there's this thing—I'm actually not allowed to go clubbing on weekdays, or, like, ever. Every now and then my parents try to act like they're responsible."

"We only party on weekdays," Ken Roberts says. "The 99 percent occupy Saturday night."

"You can tell your parents you're staying over at my house," Ken Hilton offers. "Say we're doing homework. We will be doing some reading, after all."

"My parents might insist on talking to yours first. They don't actually care, but it's important to them that other parents think they do."

"Not a problem. As long as I don't tell my dad when my mom buys a new pair of shoes she lies for me whenever I want. And as long as I don't tell my mom that my dad has already given the same pair to his medical assistant he pays off my credit card. So you see, Ken, you must come. The drugs are on daddy!"

"You're so lucky, Ken. I wish my daddy was my real daddy," Ken Roberts says.

"You're adopted?" Tommy asks.

Ken Roberts laughs. "How amazing would it be if your sugar daddy could adopt you?! I hate my parents. I wish they were dead, and not just for the tragic storyline in my future Hollywood biopic."

"You know the camera puts on ten pounds, right?" Ken Hilton says.

"There's a filter for that." Ken Roberts shrugs Ken Hilton off, but drops his fork on his tray. "So, Ken Hilton," he says in an overly eager attempt to win back favor. "Aren't you gagging over the new mall? Guess what it's going to be called?"

"Plastic Place," Tommy blurts out.

"How did *you* know?" Ken Roberts asks suspiciously.

"Oh, I just heard a rumor," Tommy says quickly. He opens a can of cream soda and takes a big gulp. Something tells him to keep Blaine to himself. Tommy hasn't forgotten how interested Ken Hilton suddenly became in their old camp counselor Derek when Tommy confessed he had a crush on him.

"My new daddy is the developer," Ken Roberts says. "He let me choose the name."

Tommy almost spits out his cream soda. Blaine's dad is Ken Roberts's latest owner? He shouldn't be surprised—everyone in Willows has a latex-coated secret . . . But, like, *wow*. Tommy's relieved he didn't mention anything about Blaine's dad or Plastic Place while he was at Ken Hilton's house, or his initiation post might be a double-feature. He scans the caf for Tutti but she's not at their usual table.

Across from him, Ken Carson is staring at his phone.

"Did you post?" Ken Hilton asks.

"Sorry, bruh, the video won't load." Ken Carson looks up. "Wi-Fi can't connect. Maybe it's, like, a sign. We should find something else to publish . . ."

"I always regret pulling your string." Ken Hilton rolls his eyes at Ken Carson. He punches the passcode into his own pink-rhinestone iPhone.

A minute later, he places the phone on the lunch table and gives Tommy a satisfied smile.

"Initiated."

Notifications ripple across tables. Everyone stops what they're doing to see the latest post on SoFamous.

The first shriek of laughter is followed by others. The cafeteria is hysterical. Ken Hilton twists a strand of his hair around his finger, already bored.

Tommy follows Ken Carson's line of vision. He's watching as Tutti walks through the doors and picks up a lunch tray. The whole cafeteria goes quiet and looks at her.

All at once, everyone breaks out into song.

I wish I were an Oscar Mayer weiner | That is what I truly wish to be | Cause if I were a Oscar Mayer weiner | Everyone would be in love | Oh everyone would be in love

Tutti drops her lunch tray.
Everyone would be in love with me.

"Yes, Ken?" Mr. Hadley says when Tommy raises his hand during chemistry. It takes Tommy a second to realize that Mr. Hadley is talking to him.

"Can I have a lavatory pass?" Tommy asks.

Mr. Hadley seems rather taken aback that a Ken is *asking* if he can leave class. Kens ditch most classes and hold court in the caf. They sometimes show up for exams, but mostly just to take a selfie of themselves taking the exam in their cutest nerd-chic outfit.

The whole class stares at Tommy as he rises from his desk and steps into the hall. Tommy feels a thrill at being the center of attention. It seems to be the only thing he's programmed to feel. Even when everyone was laughing at Tutti in the cafeteria, Tommy had felt a strange content-ment. It's not that he wanted to see Tutti humiliated, but he was just so consumed with the fact that Midge and some of the other cheerleaders were openly coveting his skin. It made his belly flip like he was on a roller coaster!

It's the only emotion he's known all day. He can't quite describe it; it's like nothing he's ever felt before. If the emotion had a name it would be *ooooooooh*. Or maybe *weeeeeeeeee*. It feels like taking whip-its while shopping really fast. Like the bubbles surrounding a cherry that has been plopped into a fizzy drink are rushing to the painted-nails emoji you have for a brain.

When someone in the hall stops to take a selfie with the new Ken:

Ooooooooh!

When someone slaps his ass in the locker room:

Weeeeeeeeee!

When Principal Elliot runs into him outside the office and asks for an autograph:

Ooooooooohweeeeeeeeeee!

The little rushes of fabulosity are tainted only by his irritated eyes. The contacts won't stop bothering him.

Inside the bathroom, Tommy checks his eyes in front of one of the mirrors. They're red as fuck. There's a rumor going around school that the new Ken comes with a Betty Ford set.

Tommy removes the contacts, staring at the reflection of Ken Rawlins. With his brown eyes, he can almost see Tommy underneath all the filler. A new emotion creeps in. Tommy suddenly misses himself. It hits him hard because it's so unexpected. For the first time, the fact that he's never coming back seems real. While he was recovering at Allan's pool house he had just been so excited about everything that was happening that it was like winning the lottery. He didn't think he'd ever come down from the high, and for the most part he hasn't. But as he stares at his reflection, he can't help wondering—is this all there is?

More waves of emotions flow through him. First, panic. Was Ken Hilton serious about sleeping with frat boys tonight at Dreamhouse?

Then isolation. Being a Ken really isn't that different from being Tommy. Sure, when he was Tommy no one even looked at him and now everyone does. But he's still alone. Even more than he was before because he doesn't have Allan or Tutti. Kens aren't exactly friends; they're more like co-stars. Most people are too intimidated by his Ken status to approach him, and even the ones who do approach do it like he's standing on an invisible pedestal. He's just as removed as ever.

And then comes the guilt. Tutti! Poor Tutti. Tommy pulls out his phone to watch the video on the post titled "Two-Ton Tutti Superstar."

A DM thread between Tutti and Ken Carson is pasted in the body of the post.

Tommy presses Play on the video Tutti sent Ken Carson. The "Oscar Mayer Wiener Song" plays in the background as Tutti performs fellatio on a hot dog. Tommy bows his head with shame. Tutti must be mortified.

"I can't decide if I really want a hot dog or if I never want to eat one again." Blaine walks into the bathroom and peers over Tommy's shoulder at the video.

"What are you doing in here?" Tommy asks.

"Relieving my bladder," Blaine says. "That okay with you?"

Tommy looks around. "Oh! I thought this was the girls' room. I must've walked in here by mistake."

"The Kens are human urinals but they don't use them, is that it?" Blaine glances back at Tommy as he takes a piss.

Tommy's burning up. What's going on? All day as a Ken he's been objectified, sent dick pics from randoms (even Jamal, the Willows High janitor), and all around treated like a piece of meat, and his heart has barely skipped a beat. But a few seconds alone with Blaine and blood is about to gush out of his ears.

As Blaine comes over to the sink to wash his hands, Tommy quickly picks up his contacts off the counter and tries to put them back in. He doesn't want Blaine to see him looking anything less than perfect.

"I like the brown better," Blaine says, turning off the tap.

"You do?" Tommy asks. "But these are the exact same shade as Ken Hilton's."

"Everyone's born with blue eyes. Before they develop enough melanin to change. They're not that special."

Tommy struggles to get one of his contacts back in. Blaine dries his hands on his jeans and holds Tommy's chin.

"Let me," he says, carefully using the tip of his finger to slide the contact into place. Tommy doesn't blink. Standing so close to Blaine has turned him as rigid as a mannequin.

Blaine doesn't remove his hand from Tommy's face right away. He touches Tommy's smooth cheek.

"No more scar," he says. "How'd you get it anyway?"

"Ken Hilton flung a burning marshmallow at me when we were kids."

"Of course he did." Blaine smirks. "Too bad it's gone, though. Made you look badass."

"More kale, sweetheart?"

Tommy accepts the bowl from his mom as they sit at the dining table.

"I'm spending the night at . . ." He hesitates. "Allan's house. We have some more studying to do."

It's easier to just lie (and easier than ever with blue eyes that only deceive) than to depend on Ken Hilton's wasted mother to cover for him tonight while he's at Dreamhouse.

"You boys." Margaret winks at Tommy.

"I'd tell you to use condoms," his dad says, "but it's not like Allan can get you pregnant!"

"George." Tommy's mom playfully swats his dad's arm. "Maybe Tommy would get Allan pregnant."

She turns to Tommy.

"Did you take your PrEP today, son?"

IN THE CLOSET

Ken Hilton's mom opens the door when Tommy pounds on the demonic knocker.

"Hey gur!" She ushers him inside. She's had so much work done since Tommy saw her last, back in elementary, that he barely recognizes her. But she doesn't recognize him either. She's so out of it she probably wouldn't recognize Tommy even if he hadn't been remodeled.

"I'm Barbara, Ken's mom," she says, giving Tommy a look-over. "*You* can call me Barbie. So hot! Ken was right about you!" Barbie hops up and down excitedly, getting hit in the face by her own beach ball boobs. "Ken's up in his room with Ken and Ken," she says. "Go ahead and join them, hunty. I'll be up in a minute and we'll do some vodka shots!" Tommy gives her a hesitant smile before climbing the stairs. "Gur, your legs are *everything*," Barbie calls after him. "Werk!"

The Kens are up in Ken Hilton's walk-in closet, sipping champagne and accessorizing.

"I think your mother just called me hunty," Tommy says from the doorway, careful not to step on any of the aristocratic bitches on the floor.

"Isn't she fabulous?" Ken Roberts asks.

"My mother is so thirsty." Ken Hilton purses his lips. He's wearing Moschino's Barbie Collection. "It's pathetic. In ten minutes she'll come in here and be all, like, 'Has anyone seen Molly?' and then laugh until she's crying because I can walk better than her in Louboutins."

"I can't wait to meet some boys tonight," Ken Roberts says. He's wearing a "Make America Great Again" red hat, which Tommy hopes is irony, though he isn't totally sure. He has seashell pasties over his nipples, paired with Daisy Dukes, threads dangling down his extremely shiny thighs. His Dippity-Do tramp stamp is accentuated with body glitter.

"I, like, put the *D* in Dreamhouse." Ken Carson checks out his reflection in the closet mirror. He's wearing a pink harness.

"What kind of guys are you into?" Ken Hilton asks Tommy. "Rich, obviously. Anything else?"

"Oh, I'm not really looking." Tommy smiles to himself, thinking of the way Blaine's hand felt against his cheek.

Ken Hilton stares at Tommy's reflection in the mirror. He lowers his bronzer brush.

"You're too new to the market to be tied down to one playmate," he says, as if reading Tommy's mind. "Slutty special features will get you on the top shelf."

Ken Roberts and Ken Carson bobble in agreement.

"Dude, is that what you're wearing?" Ken Carson asks.

"Of course not!" Ken Hilton says. "Ken Rawlins looks ratchet on purpose. He knows the best part of having a new doll is getting to dress her up." Ken Hilton squints his eyes at Tommy. "My waist is, like, 4.5 inches, but my leggings should stretch," he says, pulling items off hangers.

Music up. It's the high-school makeover montage you've been waiting for.

Each piece of fashion Ken Hilton selects is trashier than the last. Tommy is put in mesh, feathers, latex and finally nothing but a sequined G-string. Ken Hilton takes photos of each of Tommy's looks and posts some choices to the @KenRawlins Instagram to measure "the peasants' reaction." Tommy can't help but be thrilled when the photo of him in the G-string gets the most red hearts.

"Too common a choice," Ken Hilton decides, tugging the G-string down Tommy's legs.

Tommy covers himself with his hands in some kind of modest reflex, but realizes he doesn't really feel self-conscious. Actually, he's not really feeling anything at all. He puts his hand on his hip and puffs out his chest. Ken Carson winks at him.

"Put on the black latex leggings and the Céline crop," Ken Hilton tells Tommy, completing the look by throwing him a pair of eight-inch platforms. "Mood as fuck," he says.

Ken Roberts does Tommy's makeup: bronzer, eyeliner and pink lips. He gets kind of trigger happy with a can of hairspray and some gets in Tommy's eyes. His contacts burn worse than ever.

"Ugh, these are killing me," he says, removing the contacts in front of the mirror and placing them on the makeup counter.

"I know what you mean, mang." Ken Carson traces his abs. "They make my eyes hella itchy."

"Grin and bear it, bitch." Ken Hilton blinks.

"I'll just give my eyes a break for a second," Tommy says.

It's the weirdest sensation, ejecting the lenses. Tommy realizes he needs air. He takes a deep breath.

"I look like I should be in a cage hanging next to a disco ball," he says, looking at his reflection and suddenly feeling so exposed.

"If someone offers you money for sex," Ken Hilton says, "I get a cut."

Ken Roberts howls. "Okay, Kris Jenner."

Right on cue, Ken Hilton's mom appears at the doorway rattling a bottle of pills, a bottle of vodka tucked under her arm.

"Do you gurs need a ride," she asks, "or are you just going to Uber?"

Barbie takes another step into the closet and almost loses her balance. One of her breast implants is definitely bigger than the other. "I'm, like, the worst mom ever! Don't kill me, but there are only four Percs left. I forgot to fill the prescription."

"Ew," Ken Hilton whines. "Mom!"

"We have to make sacrifices sometimes, Ken," Barbie says.

"Sacrifices are for poor people. Or rich people, if they're sacrificing poor people."

Ken Hilton's mom passes them each a pill.

"You're, like, a consummate host." Ken Roberts pops his in his mouth.

Barbie offers Tommy one and he shakes his head. "That's okay, I'm not on Percocet."

"Neither are we," Ken Hilton says. "Does it look like we're snorting it? Baphomet, Ken. If you don't snort it, it's just like taking fish oil or some shit." He passes Tommy the bottle of vodka to swallow it down with, watching to make sure he takes a generous sip.

In the corner of the closet, Ken Hilton's mom is all over Ken Carson.

"Look at you, Ken!" She drools. "I swear, every time I see you those pecs are bigger!"

"Mother, you're embarrassing me," Ken Hilton says. "It's rude to be so touchy unless you're a drag queen."

Barbie growls like a cat at Ken Carson before climbing off his chest.

"Okay, get together," she says. "I'll take a photo! #squad-goals!" She uses Ken Hilton's iPhone to take a series of shots.

The Kens' poses are automatic—it's like their bodies' way of breathing. Tommy tries to keep up with each new flash, but feels like he's failing miserably. He's relieved when Ken Hilton has had enough and grabs the phone from his mother's hand, swiping through the photos with furious speed. He silently passes the phone back to Barbie.

"Ken switch place with Ken," he says, returning to his position.

"But dude, I'm always on your left," Ken Carson says.

"Not you, Ken." Ken Hilton sighs. "You, Ken. Switch with Ken."

"Me?" Ken Roberts look at Tommy. "And *her*?"

"No, the other Ken and Ken. Yes, you!"

"But *I'm* always on your right."

"Get to the edge of the photo, Ken Roberts," Ken Hilton says without sacrificing his pose for even a second. "You're simply too fat to stand next to me. My mother can't get Ken Rawlins in the frame."

Ken Roberts looks like Ken Hilton just dick slapped him a little *too* hard. But he doesn't dare put up a fight; he just silently switches places with Tommy, who tries to distract himself from his growing anxiety by focusing on his poses.

"Don't you know your new angles yet?" Ken Hilton looks up from his phone at Tommy as he swipes through the retakes.

"Can I see?" Ken Roberts comes back to life.

Ken Hilton ghosts him.

"Now we party," he says.

They shuffle out of Ken Hilton's closet so abruptly that Tommy forgets his blue contacts on the makeup counter.

DREAMHOUSE

Tommy grips the sides of the passenger seat of Ken Hilton's Corvette. When they left Ken Hilton's house, Ken Roberts practically flew out the door and up to the car yelling "Shotgun!" but Ken Hilton made him sit in the backseat with Ken Carson. When Ken Roberts tried to argue, Ken Hilton snapped, "Unless you'd rather I tie you up—"

Ken Roberts's eyes lit up.

"And drag you by the back of my car," Ken Hilton finished.

The Percocet and vodka have gone straight to Tommy's head. He's kind of nauseous, especially as Ken Hilton makes turns without slowing down. The wind whipping through the top of the convertible has absolutely no effect on their hair.

They fly to Dreamhouse, coming down a hill like it's a rainbow. Tommy's veneers are chattering as he steps out of the car.

"Dude, what's wrong with you?" Ken Carson asks.

"Yeah," Ken Roberts says. "You're not overdosing already, are you?"

"No," Tommy says quickly. "I'm just cold. Does anyone have a sweater?"

"A what?" Ken Hilton recoils.

Tommy can't help but notice Ken Roberts smiling, like he's sure Ken Hilton is about to rip off one of Tommy's limbs.

"We never wear sweaters," Ken Hilton says. "Think of all the skin they'd cover!"

"Right." Tommy suppresses a shiver. "Duh."

They bypass the line outside. The bouncer gives Ken Hilton a reverent nod of his head before lifting the velvet rope.

The Kens make their grand entrance. Jazzie, Dreamhouse's resident DJ, plays "Money, Success, Fame, Glamour" when he spots them. The whole club is watching.

Tommy stands next to Ken Hilton and mimics his pose— hand on jutting hip, gooey blow-up mouth spread into a dazzling, hateful smile.

Ken Roberts is already being passed a shot by an admiring daddy, and Ken Carson does a spin around a go-go pole. The queens go wild for him.

As they walk through the club toward the VIP section, Tommy feels self-conscious with everyone staring. He wobbles in his platforms. They're too small and the strap is cutting off the circulation in his foot. He takes another step and face-plants. People see. It's bad. There's definitely a Snapchat story. Ken Hilton pretends it's not happening and keeps walking. Tommy is helped up by a drag queen who breathes her coke breath all over his face and introduces herself as Diana Wails. "Now give Auntie a kiss," she says, slobbering all over Tommy's face.

Tommy manages to pull away and shrink into the Kens' booth.

Ken Hilton side-eyes him. "Can you walk?"

Someone sends over a bottle of Veuve Clicquot and Tommy takes a sip, trying to collect himself. The glass shakes in his hand. The club is so hot, and he feels so ridiculous. Tommy didn't think a Ken could sweat, but his crop-top has crescent sweat marks under the armpits. He tries to position his body so that Ken Hilton won't notice.

Tommy has seen countless photos of Dreamhouse on SoFamous, but they can't compare to actually being inside. It's styled after Jayne Mansfield's iconic Hollywood mansion, the Pink Palace. The VIP room is floor to ceiling pink shag carpet. The dance floor is covered in foam and diamonds. Tommy wonders if there really is a heart-shaped Jacuzzi in the dark room . . .

"Ugh." Ken Roberts looks around. "There's, like, no one here tonight. Will I never meet my dream man in Dreamhouse?"

"You mean a dildo with a black card?" Ken Hilton asks.

Ken Carson crackles. "Read as fuck, bruh."

"My mama always said reading is good for your imagination," Ken Roberts says, "something that go-go in those Rocky shorts obviously doesn't have. Look at his dancing! He's moving like he's in the Manchester arena bombing."

"Dude, look at that drag queen at the bar." Ken Carson points to an obese seven-foot-tall man in a dress. "She can't get a twink to stuff, so she stuffs twinkies!"

"Okay, NuKen." Ken Hilton turns to Tommy. "Your turn. Pick a book, any book."

"I don't know." Tommy hesitates. "I don't really have anything mean to say about anyone."

"We're not being mean," Ken Hilton insists. "We're reading."

"Dude, what's the difference again?" Ken Carson asks.

"Duh," Ken Hilton says. "Reading is fundamental."

"We'll make it easy for you." Ken Roberts motions toward the DJ booth.

Tommy looks over at a guy dancing to Top 40 music.

"Um," Tommy says, finally blurting out, "is this a theme party, because that choker is so '90s!"

"Original, bruh," Ken Carson says.

Ken Hilton's champagne glass almost shatters in his hand.

"Ken Roberts just gave you SJP on a silver platter. With that horse face all you had to do was neigh!"

"What does SJP stand for?" Tommy asks.

"Sarah Jessica Parker, dude." Ken Carson bows his head.

Ken Hilton looks away from him in a way that leaves Tommy feeling like he no longer exists.

Three muscle jocks with overly tweezed eyebrows come over to their booth. They each wear a tank top in a different pastel color. Ken Hilton seems to know the one wearing pink. At least he sits on his lap like he does. But then Tommy overhears them exchange names and realizes they've just met. Ken Roberts and Ken Carson begin making out with Yellow Tank Top, and Purple slides closer to Tommy.

"Bump?" he asks, offering Tommy the powdered tip of a key.

"No thanks," Tommy says. His head is already pounding.

Ken Hilton overhears Tommy's refusal. "Don't be rude," he says, leaning over and taking the bump himself.

"Ken, I'm not feeling so hot." Tommy fans himself with a cocktail napkin. "I think I'm going to be sick."

"Stick a dick in your mouth." Ken Hilton goes back to making out with Pink Tank Top.

"I might be able to help you with that," Purple Tank Top offers. He pulls Tommy close to his rock-hard chest and chokes him with his tongue.

Tommy squirms. He isn't able to pull away fast enough. He feels a burning in his stomach. Before he can stop it, puke spews out of his mouth and lands all over Purple Tank Top.

Ken Roberts starts dry heaving at the sight of the puke. He's worked his gag reflex into submission; all he has to do is think of vomit and it starts coming up. He runs off to the bathroom.

The tank top boys quickly ditch the VIP section. Ken Hilton tries to stop them from going but ends up slipping on Tommy's puke and collapsing on the floor. The vom on his Moschino flashes under the strobe light.

As the club spins around him, Tommy asks for water.

"What did you just say?" Ken Hilton asks.

"Water," Tommy croaks.

He can't focus his eyes, but he can *feel* Ken Hilton's glare slicing through him. And then he remembers, the only water the Kens drink is during water sports . . .

The entire club is looking over at them, taking in the image of the Kens surrounded by vomit and not a single cute guy. Ken Hilton grabs Tommy and drags him so hard through the club his arm almost pops out of its socket. Tommy stumbles through the backdoor of Dreamhouse out into the alley.

He pukes the rest of his stomach contents out behind the Dumpster. He stands up straight and focuses his eyes. Ken Hilton is recording him with his iPhone.

"That's it," Ken Hilton hisses. "You are so *over*. I don't know why I thought I could be friends with the fat poor kid. You're hopeless! I'm taking you out of the display window and putting you back in the box where you're going to rot, thot."

Ken Hilton goes close-up on Tommy's smudged eyeliner.

"The swan goes back to being an ugly duckling. I can't take back your surgeries, but I'll have your new nose broken if you so much as look at me again."

"What?" Tommy can barely register what's happening.

"I really wanted you to be something," Ken Hilton says. "But it has become painfully clear that you are beyond help." He shakes his head. "I was so wrong about you! I just can't help but take pity on a basic bitch every now and then. I always regret being nice. Will I never learn?"

"Ken, I'm sorry! I just don't feel well . . . I don't really drink."

"Or gossip or do coke or know how to accessorize for shit," Ken Hilton adds. "I bet if that guy in there had asked you for a blow job you would have given him the number of your cheap fucking hairstylist!"

"Why are you being such a cunt?" Tommy asks. "I need to go home. I drank too much. I should sleep it off."

"Do you even hear yourself?" Ken Hilton rattles. "We haven't even gone to the after-party yet!"

"Please don't do this again." Tommy holds on to himself. "I thought we were friends."

"You are, like, so obsessed with me," Ken Hilton says. "Since you need another reading lesson, allow me to give you one, *Thomas*. You're such a loser, all the followers I bought you unfollowed."

"Yeah, well . . . ," Tommy stammers. "Your mom is her own season of *Botched*!"

"For your information, she likes it when people stare!" Ken Hilton holds up his iPhone. "Just wait for your eulogy post," he says.

Ken Hilton yanks the stud out of Tommy's left ear. Tommy gasps in shock.

"Diamonds are forever"—Ken Hilton tosses the earring in the air and catches it in his palm—"but *your* time is up."

PART 3

COLLECTIBLES

"You live or die with the quality of the projection you make."

RUTH HANDLER

DECONSTRUCTION

The magic bleeds out of him.

Tommy steadies himself by holding on to the Dumpster. He brings his hand to his ear to see if his lobe is split. It throbs, but still seems to be in one piece.

The bass from the music inside Dreamhouse pounds through the backdoor. *Some dream!*

He limps to the end of the alley in Ken Hilton's platforms. At the street, he stops and looks both ways. He doesn't know where he's going, but he has to move. He wants to get as far away from Ken Hilton and his insanity as possible. Off-screen, evil isn't so glamorous.

The Kens may be plastic, but inside they're pure acid.

A wave of regret suddenly washes over Tommy as he keeps walking. Has he really been kicked out of Ken World already? He feels defective. Was this Ken Hilton's plan the entire time? To give Tommy everything only for the amusement of taking it away? It all feels so familiar.

The cold makes him shiver. Maybe it was the booze, or the Percocet, or the way he could tell that Purple Tank Top was uncircumcised under his jeans . . . but it was just too much for him.

All the horrible things Ken Hilton said swirl in Tommy's mind. He'd been completely degraded, and didn't even have red ass cheeks to show for it!

Tommy had always known the Kens were a void—that was part of their appeal. They didn't feel, or think, or worry like everyone else. They were so empty that they floated above all the mundanities of life. They didn't need to eat, shit or even breathe. They were fueled by a lack of substance. And once Tommy had entered the void, he felt like a mannequin who came to life after closing but was never able to leave the store.

It's a wonder he'd made it out alive. Being a Ken wasn't nearly as fun as reading about them on Tumblr. You can only replace food with bitchiness for so long. Unless you're as depraved as Ken Hilton, it simply isn't sustainable.

A gas station is up the street. Tommy turns into the parking lot and walks up to his reflection in the glass window. He doesn't look at himself in the same obsessive way he has ever since his transformation. This time, he stares at his reflection in the glossed gas station window, trying to see if somewhere beyond the plastic he still exists.

Tommy doesn't hear the bells on the gas station door ringing, or footsteps coming up beside him.

"Looking a little worse for wear, Ken." Blaine sucks on the straw of a slushy.

Tommy had been so consumed with his sudden fall from Ken that he hadn't noticed the Harley in the parking lot.

"I'm not a Ken anymore," he says.

"Has your soul reentered your body?"

"I feel like shit, so I guess so."

Blaine takes a loud slurp of his slushy. He motions for Tommy to sit next to him on the curb and offers him a sip from the straw. It soothes Tommy's raw throat.

"Not as seen in commercials?" Blaine asks.

"It literally made me vomit."

"You hurled?"

"And Ken Hilton filmed it." Tommy buries his face in his hands. "It wasn't even fun! I think that's what I'm the most disappointed about. There were moments where I felt as carefree as the Kens. It was horrible, but wonderful, being so selfish. Loving yourself so much. But I couldn't make it last. I just couldn't stop feeling. Except when . . ." Tommy blinks. "Except when I was wearing the Kens' contacts. Isn't that weird? When they were in I felt invincible. They were irritating my eyes so I took them out while we were getting ready for Dreamhouse, and I forgot to put them back in before we left. Maybe that's why I was such a mess. With the contacts, I saw everything from above it all. Without them, I was just . . . me."

Tommy wipes the dust off the knees of his leggings. "I gave up myself to walk the hallway like a catwalk with the Kens, only to realize that the catwalk doesn't lead where I thought it did. And if you dare lose step, the drop is steep."

"Sounds like they need to be tripped," Blaine says.

"The Kens are impenetrable."

"I bet if everyone stopped kissing Ken Hilton's Brazilian butt lift he'd land on it." Blaine jumps to a stand and gives Tommy his hand. "Let's get that ear cleaned up," he says.

At the end of a cul-de-sac in The Hills sits Blaine's traditional house with powder-blue shutters. They park the bike in the driveway and go around back. The first glow of sunrise behind the hills gives the sky a metallic sheen that reflects off the surface of a pool.

Blaine takes off his leather jacket and drops it to the grass. He starts pulling off his shirt.

"What are you doing?" Tommy asks.

"I told you we'd get that ear cleaned up." Blaine kicks off his boots. When he pulls down his jeans and stars-and-stripes boxers, Tommy doesn't know where to look. His eyes land on a tattoo on Blaine's thigh—the grim reaper carrying a scythe and standing beside a girl with her arm around his cloak. A speech balloon says, "I've always been a sucker for a man in uniform!"

Blaine cannonballs into the water, splashing Tommy's legs.

"Get in!" he yells as he resurfaces.

Tommy stretches Ken Hilton's crop-top as he pulls it over his head, careful to avoid his ear. The leggings are stuck to his skin with sweat; it takes him forever to pull them off. He hops around and almost falls over. He can hear Blaine laughing at him.

As soon as he's naked, Tommy jumps straight into the pool. He's suddenly self-conscious again. It had felt fine being naked in front of the Kens earlier, but he's shy with Blaine.

The water is warm. Tommy's ear stings in the chlorine, but the pain is a relief. It's the part of him that's still real.

Tommy swims around Blaine, their legs grazing under the surface. It's so electric that it's like the sunrise is lifting from directly beneath them. The surface of the water flashes like a silvery sheet of light, whiting out their faces as they swim over to the end of the infinity pool. They're all wet lips and wet eyelashes and wet dreams.

"So it ends." Tommy leans his head against the edge of the pool. "Now that I've seen what goes on behind the shelf I feel like such an idiot. Ken Hilton should seriously be stopped. Ken Roberts wouldn't be so insecure if he wasn't always in Ken Hilton's shadow. And I can tell Ken Carson isn't really a bully. That's why he always seems so relieved when he can escape on the football field. There'd be no Kens without Ken Hilton. Just think how different school would be."

"It's not just school. This town is everything that's wrong with the world. It's like a never-ending E! special." Blaine shudders. "I overheard these two moms pushing strollers on the street talking about taking their babies to get their first shot—of Botox."

Tommy swallows some pool water. He wonders how much Blaine knows about his dad and Ken Roberts.

"Sometimes it's even worse at home than on the streets . . . ," Tommy says.

"Yeah." Blaine snorts. "My dad's swallowed the glitter pill. But I know my mom would have been able to see through this place."

"Where is she?"

Blaine stares at Tommy as blankly as the Kens. It makes the heated pool suddenly feel freezing.

"Force Quit," Blaine finally says. He jumps out of the pool. "Is it true Ken Hilton lives nearby?" he asks. "My dad says Hilton House is a real work of art."

"It's a few blocks away," Tommy says. "Why?"

"I've been meaning to ask if he wants to come out and play . . ."

Blaine goes into the pool house and grabs two towels. He brings one to Tommy as he climbs out of the water.

"It's almost time for school." Tommy looks at the sunrise as he dries his hair. "And I left my clothes at Ken Hilton's house! He wanted to dress me up."

"No problem." Blaine wraps his towel around his waist. "I'll lend you something. But we should still swing by Ken Hilton's house to pick up your stuff on the way to school."

"What for?"

"We could be the ones to dismantle the pillar of blond. Of course, the whole town will probably end up smothered."

"I don't know," Tommy says. "I just want to avoid the Kens . . ."

Blaine digs through the pocket of his leather jacket, still lying on the ground, and pulls out his phone.

"You're not going to let Ken Hilton discard you like a broken toy, are you?" he asks. Blaine shows Tommy his phone. "Just as I suspected. Ken Hilton sure didn't waste any time."

The tab on the phone is open to SoFamous, where a headline reads: "Ken Rawlins's Eulogy Post." Blaine clicks Play and he and Tommy watch a wobbly Tommy retching in the alley behind Dreamhouse.

"I'm taking you out of the display window and putting you back in the box where you're going to rot, thot," Ken Hilton hisses.

Tommy hits Stop.

"That bitch!"

FACE OFF

Tommy borrows a pair of gym shorts and a Supreme hoodie from Blaine for the ride to Ken Hilton's house. Blaine also gives him a pair of sneakers so that he doesn't have to wear Ken Hilton's hooker heels. His club clothes are in a bag. Tommy is dressed before Blaine is ready; he says he has to gather the "supplies." Tommy's too distracted by the fact that he's alone in Blaine's room to question what he means. He sits on the edge of the bed, running his hands along the sheets. There's a Charles Manson poster hanging on the closet door with his quote, "We're not in Wonderland anymore, Alice."

"Tell me about it," Tommy says to himself.

When they pull up to Hilton House, the gate is closed. Blaine parks the bike and they climb over the hedges. The sun has fully risen in the sky, and rays of light are shining through the fountain at the center of the driveway.

"You think anyone's up?" Blaine asks.

"Even if his mom's home, she won't notice us," Tommy says. "She's played by Tara Reid."

Blaine checks the door. It's unlocked. Before opening it all the way, he gives Tommy a quick smirk. It's totally his signature sculpt, with his eyebrows arching into triangles on his forehead.

They step into the house. Tommy's scared that if Ken Hilton catches them he'll be the subject of another post on SoFamous, this time bumping Coach Summers as Ken Hilton's stalker. (Coach Summers said good morning to Ken Hilton one day before Ken Hilton had acknowledged him.)

"I'll just leave the clothes here for the maid," Tommy says, dropping the bag on a table next to a bouquet of pink roses with buds that look like the tips of Barbie's shoes. "Forget revenge. Let's just get out of here." Tommy turns toward the door, but Blaine holds him back.

"Don't you want to give Ken Hilton some of his own medicine?" he asks.

A loud snore comes from the living room. Blaine brings his index finger to his lips. They creep down the hall and find Ken Hilton's mom passed out on the floor, drooling onto a Birkin pillow. At first Tommy panics, thinking that she's awake—her eyes are partway open—but her face is just pulled so tight she can't fully close them.

"What's she on?" Blaine asks.

"Everything," Tommy whispers. "Haven't you seen Ken Hilton's 'Pill of the Day' posts on SoFamous? I swear I learn more about chemistry from his mother's medicine cabinet than in class."

Tommy leads Blaine to the kitchen. If he remembers correctly from his childhood, Barbie Hilton's stash is in the cabinet above the sink. He and Blaine stand back in awe. Lined up are row after row of prescription pill bottles.

"Vicodin, OxyContin, Roxycodone, Percocet . . ." Blaine reads the labels on the bottles. "Ooh, Flintstone vitamins!" He pops the lid and tosses one in his mouth.

Blaine grabs another bottle, opening the lid and dumping the white pills into the trash.

"We have to get Ken where it'll really hurt," he says. "His vanity."

"How?" Tommy asks.

Blaine slides his backpack off his shoulders and starts pulling out supplies.

"I stocked up right after I saw you at Allan's pool house," Blaine says, taking off his leather jacket and rolling up the sleeves of his shirt. He reaches for the aluminum powder. "You can pass Ken the bottle, pretending you're trying to make amends. New on the market. An unreal high."

"But Allan said you should detonate in an open field! We don't want to kill him . . ."

Tommy searches the side of Blaine's face. Blaine keeps measuring the potassium perchlorate.

"Don't worry, it'll just blow enough to singe Ken Hilton's plastic." He stops pouring and glances over at Tommy. "Kinda like what he did to you."

The spot on Tommy's face where his scar used to be starts burning.

"Well, as long as DeepFace can still recognize him," Tommy says.

Blaine had even packed a drill to make a hole in the lid. He sticks a safety fuse through it and pops the lid back on the bottle.

"Which way to Her Royal Highness's room?" he asks, hanging his jacket around his shoulders.

When they enter Ken Hilton's boudoir, the dogs jump off the bed and run over to them. The tiny barks don't wake Ken Hilton. You have to switch him on to wake him up. He remains asleep, surrounded by dolls and teddy bears, looking immaculate despite last night's wild antics. That's just like Ken Hilton. When he should have a hangover from hell he jumps out of bed in the morning looking flawless and is all, "Bonjour, bitches!"

Blaine walks around Ken Hilton's bed to the nightstand. He picks up a key and a bag of cocaine next to the Hello Kitty alarm clock, scoops up a generous bump and puts it under Ken Hilton's nose. Ken Hilton breathes it up with a gentle snore and his eyes instantly fling open. His eyeliner is perfect. Not even a little smudged. Like he reapplied it right before passing out.

"What the *actual* fuck?" Ken Hilton shoots into a sitting position.

"Morning, doll face," Blaine says.

Ken Hilton looks from Tommy to Blaine. "What are you two doing here?"

"I brought your clothes back," Tommy says.

"You can keep my puke-stained Céline, thanks." Ken Hilton gets out of bed and puts on a pink housecoat with feathered trim. "Actually, I'm glad you're here. I can finish the excommunication by shaving off your blond."

"Good thing you didn't let him dye your pubes, right Tommy?" Blaine laughs.

"You've seen his pubes?" Ken Hilton stares at Blaine. "I thought the Virgin Mary over here was afraid of a little cock."

"Sorry I'm not enough of a whore for you," Tommy says, finally gaining the courage to stand up to Ken Hilton. "I guess I'm not meant to be an A-gay."

"No, you're too much of a gay-gay."

"Why are you so ripe, Ken?" Tommy's voice is shaking with rage. "I don't expect we can be friends but—"

"Friends?" Ken Hilton forces a laugh. "Facebook only lets you have five thousand friends."

"Salty," Blaine says. "Tommy here came to make amends. He even brought a peace offering."

Blaine shows Ken Hilton the pill bottle. A carefully placed finger conceals the fuse.

"What are those?" Ken Hilton asks.

"They light you on fire," Tommy says.

Ken Hilton rolls his eyes. "I don't need your Tic Tacs."

He turns to one of his mirrored walls and runs his hand through his hair.

"I knew he wouldn't take one." Blaine tilts his head at Tommy. "He probably just posts about being a pillhead for Likes."

"Get fucked." Ken Hilton pries himself away from his reflection. "Any vodka to chase them with?"

Tommy sees Blaine discreetly use a lighter on the bomb behind his back. The fuse sparks. Blaine passes Ken Hilton the bottle and grabs Tommy's arm, quickly pulling him back to the far mirrored wall. Blaine covers their heads with his leather jacket.

By the time Ken Hilton realizes there's a burning fuse attached to the lid, it's too late.

"Ew" is his last word.

SUICIDE POST

The bottle explodes. A roar of hot wind slams against Blaine's jacket. Ken Hilton's face melts off. Smoke lifts from his burning hair. A teacup Pomeranian barks.

Ken Hilton is still clutching the bottle with a charred hand as he collapses to the floor.

Tommy comes out from underneath the jacket and clamps his hand over his mouth.

Blaine goes up to the body and stomps out the flames burning the feathered trim of Ken Hilton's housecoat.

The bedroom reeks like burning plastic.

A chunk of Ken Hilton's filler has glommed onto a mirrored wall. It falls to the floor, landing with a plop. One of the Pomeranians wobbles over in its heavy collar and eats it. Tommy feels faint.

"I thought you said it would be a small explosion?!"

"Didn't take us down, did it?" Blaine says.

Tommy genuflects for Ken Hilton one last time—his knees buckle. It's a good thing there's nothing left in his stomach after last night or he'd be sick. What remains of Ken Hilton's face looks like a pizza pie with no cheese.

"He doesn't have a pulse," Tommy says, lifting the limp wrist of Ken Hilton's unburned hand. "But that doesn't mean anything, right? Ken Hilton was always heartless." Then, overcome by shock, he collapses against the side of the bed, clutching his knees to his chest.

"We killed Ken!"

"Trust me," Blaine says, "guys like Ken Hilton are Hydras. You cut off one head and two more pop up in its place."

"Murrica," Tommy murmurs. He isn't blinking, like a doll that only closes its eyes when it's lying down.

Blaine starts pacing the room. "What are we going to tell the police?" he asks.

Tommy's unblinking eyes widen.

"The police? Can't we just report it to Facebook?"

"Maybe we don't have to go to the police. When celebrities die there's always a lot of talk, right? Was it murder? Was it an Illuminati assassination? Or . . . was it suicide?"

"Suicide?" Tommy stares at the dead body. "Like, what is life?"

"Don't act like you aren't thrilled."

"What is that supposed to mean?" Tommy shoots to a standing position. "I thought Willows High would be better off without Ken Hilton, but I never wanted him to die! I just wanted him to stop being retweeted, which he'd consider infinitely worse."

Blaine walks over to Ken Hilton's pink-rhinestone iPhone; it's sitting on top of his nightstand, next to the alarm clock and bag of blow.

"You always wanted to post like Ken. Now's your chance."

He passes Tommy the phone. "We could make it look like Ken Hilton sent himself to meet his maker."

"The Pink Power Ranger and Darth Vader?" Tommy asks. "Maybe that is the best solution under the circumstances. It was an accident . . ."

"Do you know the password?"

"Fifty-one fifty," Tommy says, flopping down on the bed. "Fifty-one fifty! Oh, think of all the things Ken Hilton will never get to do."

Tommy types in the password and clicks the pink KKK app, opening a SoFamous template. It takes him a second to think of what to write, but once he starts it flows. Getting into Ken Hilton's head isn't difficult. There's lots of room.

"I'm sure this will come as a shock, but I always did make you gag," Tommy reads as he types. "I thought I'd join the twenty-seven club, but once again I'm ahead of the trend . . ."

"Motive," Blaine says. "Why would Ken Hilton kill himself?"

"Well, he was just complaining about Brad Curtis cheating on him with Francie Fairchild . . ."

"When you're bad you're so good." Blaine nods encouragingly. Tommy keeps typing.

"You may think that because I'm the most popular kid in school, gorgeous and rich, that I have it all. But too much of everything is never enough. Fans aren't friends, old people all have pillow face, and you can't pay to mend a broken heart. My boyfriend is in love with another woman. I'm melting."

"I'd Like it," Blaine says.

Tommy publishes the post before he loses his nerve, quickly tossing the phone across the bed. He's anticipating another explosion.

Comments section about to blow.

FAKE HOLLYWOOD STORY

Willows High is abuzz when Tommy and Blaine pull up to the parking lot on Blaine's motorcycle. The whole school is talking about Ken Hilton's latest post. The rumor mill is out of control.

Ken Hilton didn't commit suicide, Russia hacked SoFamous.

Ken Hilton faked his own death and will reappear as a woman after surgery. It's so obviously a publicity stunt, like back when Ken Hilton posted a Snapchat wearing a brunette wig and everyone had a collective heart attack.

Ken Hilton will rise again, and only the blond will be saved.

Everyone reminisces about their favorite Ken Hilton memory. Like that time he spent $10,000 on the world's smallest puppy, which he named Empress Ken Hilton. He tied it by a leash to the rearview mirror of his Corvette. All day long everyone kept going to the parking lot to take photos of the dog, even after it had died from heat stroke.

Or that time he drove over Principal Elliot and Principal Elliot apologized to *him*.

No one at Willows High can believe the queen is dead. The flag at the front of the school is lowered to half-mast. Everyone's glued to their phone. There's a storm of status updates, each more overly emotional and self-involved than the last. Ken Hilton's STARmeter rises. You're always a hotter topic in death, especially when you're going to hell.

The Willows High student body mourns Ken Hilton by Sharing him. But no one is actually sad that he's dead. Ken Hilton's death doesn't even really penetrate. It's all surface level, the drama of the moment appearing on their feeds like a terrorist attack or school shooting. Soon they'll get bored and scroll past it, onto Taylor's new video.

Tommy is in such a daze as he walks into the locker room for P.E. that he doesn't even register Ken Roberts sitting on a bench eating McDonald's nuggets.

"Dude, be careful," Ken Carson tells Ken Roberts from his locker. "You're ruining your chance of making the *Guinness Book of World Records* for not digesting anything but come for a whole year."

"Oh, let Ken Hilton keep it." Ken Roberts bites into a piece of chicken. "He always said he peaked in the fifth grade."

Ken Carson closes his locker and notices Tommy.

"You're lucky Ken Hilton is dead, bruh," he says. "He wanted us to hang you from the flag pole by ramming it up your ass."

Ken Roberts licks his fingers. "And I was, like, how is that a punishment?"

"Spill the tea, dude," Ken Carson says. "Did you kill Ken Hilton?"

"What?" Tommy's face turns white. "Why would you say that?"

"He was pretty upset after you left, bruh. He had to hate-fuck all the bartenders at Dreamhouse to calm himself down."

"Hella pissed." Ken Roberts bobbles, chewing with his mouth open. "And bendy."

"Dude, he had high hopes that he could make you somebody," Ken Carson says. "Maybe the disappointment drove him to suicide."

"'Zif." Ken Roberts burps. "Ken Hilton wouldn't kill himself over some knock-off. He obviously just did it for attention." He picks up his phone with sticky fingers. "It just isn't fair! His stats are blowing up!" He throws the phone against the lockers.

"Ken, that's, like, the tenth phone you've broken this year," Ken Carson says.

"Ken, I can't help it if all my personal assistants suck!"

Tommy leans his head against a locker, hitting it over and over. The Restylane prevents him from feeling a thing.

"Are you, like, breaking down, Ken?" Ken Carson asks.

"You just called him Ken, Ken," Ken Roberts says.

"Well, Ken," Ken Carson says, "with Ken being all, like, dead and shit, shouldn't we consider keeping him a Ken?"

"Why would we do that, Ken?"

"Because there's supposed to be three Kens, Ken. We can't just leave an empty space on the shelf. What if it gets finessed?"

"You might be right, Ken."

Ken Carson turns to Tommy. "Dude, you can still sit with us."

"But put in your contacts, pronto!" Ken Roberts adds.

Tommy stops hitting his head.

"No," he says.

The two Kens stare at him blankly. They've never heard that word before.

"Dude, *what*?" Ken Carson asks.

"I said no! The whole point was to end the Kens, to make Willows High a nicer school." Tommy slams his mouth shut, worried he's said too much. But his words don't even register with the Kens. *Nice* stumps them almost as much as *no*.

"Don't you want a fresh start?" Tommy asks. "A school without all the pressure of Ken?"

"Pressure is good," Ken Roberts says. "It takes pressure to make diamonds."

"This is our chance!" Tommy insists. "With Ken Hilton off the screen, we can transform Willows High."

"Ken Hilton isn't off the screen, bruh. My feed is wall-papered with posts about him."

Ken Carson shows Tommy his phone.

"If Ken Hilton knew how famous he'd be after killing himself, he would've done it a long time ago."

Without Ken Hilton at the helm, no one knows at what speed to run laps around the gym. Ken Carson steps up to the plate and sets the pace. It's faster than the class is used to. Ken Hilton just sort of floated around the gym, his feet never fully touching the floor, but Ken Carson runs like he's surfing a fast-moving wave.

Tommy, Allan and Tutti can't keep up. They slow to a walk. They'd come together at the start of gym class. Tommy thought they might blame him for the "Two-Ton Tutti Superstar" post, but in the wake of Ken Hilton's death, that no longer seems to matter. None of them say a word. Tommy is afraid of speaking because he's sure they know him well enough to tell by the sound of his voice that something is up; Tutti is totally stunned; and Allan is just being respectful of the dead. Everyone else can't stop talking about Ken Hilton, and they hear bits and pieces of conversation as the class whizzes by.

"I like your shirt." Tommy is the first to break the silence; he can't stand it anymore. Allan is wearing a graphic tee that has an image of a hand holding up a middle finger. The text above it reads, "Accept that I don't want to be like you."

"You do?" Allan asks.

"And not just because I saw a photo in *Star* magazine of Sofia Richie wearing it," Tommy says.

"Is this your way of saying you regret becoming a Ken?"

"We saw the eulogy post." Tutti looks at him apologetically. "Ken Hilton's last post. Wow."

"I guess I never really got over Ken Hilton," Tommy says. "He was the first friend I ever made, and after he ditched me, I just felt like there was something wrong with me. But there's something wrong with the Kens—with this town made in their image—not me. I wanted to be a part of the beautiful sheeple because they're beautiful, but I failed to realize they're also sheep . . ."

Blaine comes out of the locker room and shares a quick look with Tommy across the gym before he starts running.

"And there are wolves out there, you know," Tommy finishes.

He links arms with Tutti.

"I'm sorry about Weinergate. I knew the Kens were up to something, I just wasn't sure what . . . but the truth is, even if I had known, I don't know if I would've tried to stop them. It was like I just stopped caring. That was the scariest part. When I wasn't totally dysfunctional as a Ken I felt this magical nothingness. It wasn't exactly Zen. Well, kind of. But instead of a Buddha it would be the Louis Vuitton logo. It was like this long exhale over a pink, perfectly still body of water. All was okay in the world. I was pretty and popular."

"It's okay, Tommy. I don't blame you. I'm the dolt who fell for Ken Carson."

"But I'm the one who let it slip that you have a crush on him."

"It's old news. Ken Hilton's suicide post has buried my little video for good."

Ken Carson runs past with Ken Roberts by his side. Tommy catches Tutti staring after him.

"If it's any consolation," he tells her, "I got the feeling Ken Carson didn't really want to go through with it."

"Maybe the Kens aren't as shallow as I thought," Allan says. "I just assumed Ken Hilton was too consumed with his reflection for self-reflection, but even he realized how superficial his life was in the end. Is it true he used a pill bomb?"

"Where did you hear that?" Tommy asks, lowering his voice as Blaine passes.

"That's what everyone's saying," Tutti says. "I just can't believe it. It really felt like Ken Hilton would always be here. Like the WILLOWSLAND sign, towering over everyone."

Ken Hilton's fame continues to grow for the rest of the day. Stacie Skipper arrives on the Willows High campus. Stacie is a reporter for *Willows News* and a recurring meme on SoFamous over a leaked and subsequently viral behind-the-scenes video of her pouring herself a glass of wine from a cube she keeps under her news desk. She downed that baby during the countdown leading up to the five o'clock news. It has spawned countless memes.

Stacie and her crew are at the school to interview students about Ken Hilton's suicide.

In death, Ken Hilton finally has depth. He'd been celebrated for his superficiality, but beneath his glossy veneer was a complicated and tormented soul. Suddenly, everyone's talking about how deep and misunderstood he was. Even his haters have a newfound respect. The Stoner Conspiracy Theorists create a video about his secret life and pain.

Tommy goes home with Blaine after school. They haven't dared speak a word to each other all day. Tommy has never been so exhausted in his life. He hadn't slept a wink the night before, and all day at school he was on edge, waiting for someone to realize what they had done. But everyone was sympathetic and lavishing him with attention—so struck by the death of Ken Hilton that they'd forgotten all about the Ken Rawlins eulogy post.

Blaine switches on the TV as he and Tommy sit on the couch to watch *Willows News*. Stacie Skipper's chipper voice fills the living room.

"I'm Stacie Skipper reporting for *Willows News* at Willows High School, which is reeling from the shock suicide of one of its most beloved students."

Stacie Skipper walks up to Francie Fairchild, who is wearing her cheer uniform. She's first in a line of students standing outside the front doors of school, thirsty for camera time.

"What's your name, dear?" Stacie asks.

"Francie Fairchild, flyer."

"Did you know Ken Hilton well?"

"Ken Hilton was the sweetest, like, nicest person ever. We were really close," Francie says with a glottal fry. "We had similar taste in . . . well, a few things. He was really androgynous, so sometimes we'd share clothes . . ."

"Francie must be thrilled." Tommy snorts. "Everyone thinks Ken Hilton killed himself because of her! Talk about a comeback."

Stacie Skipper walks down the line to interview more students. She stops at one of the Barks.

"I can't believe Ken's gone," he says. "He was always trying to make the world a better place. Like, he organized a blood-diamond drive all by himself."

"I don't know who's more disgusting," Blaine says, "Ken Hilton or the vermin who made him."

"Look at the people lining up to sanctify him." Tommy runs his hand through his hair; it's brittle and lifeless without Dippity-Do. "Was I really that delusional?"

Tommy uses the remote to mute the TV. He turns to face Blaine.

"I think we should talk."

Blaine gives him a look. "Don't make me take out your batteries."

It doesn't matter who laughs first. Once they start, they can't stop. Tommy leans back on the couch, laughing so hard tears are streaming down his cheeks and Stacie Skipper's shoulder pads become a blur.

OVER YOUR DEAD BODY

On the Facebook event page for Ken Hilton's funeral it says to wear pink.

Tommy wears a pink tie. Blaine sits next to him in a pew at Famous Family dressed all in black, but chewing Hubba Bubba and blowing bubbles, if that counts.

Ken Hilton's mom is sitting in the front wearing a pink veil. Dr. Hilton has his head bowed as if in prayer—but he's really just checking Tinder.

Father Dude approaches the podium.

"Today we commemorate the life of Ken Hilton," he says, finding his light through the stained-glass windows. "Ken Hilton was a viral sensation, blond mafia don and the seed of his father's scalpel. An immaculate son of sodomy. He was perfect. But what does that mean in an imperfect world? May Ken Hilton's death serve as a reminder to the YouTube generation that the most important channel to subscribe to is God's. Do *you* follow?"

One by one, those packing the church go up to Ken Hilton's casket to say goodbye. Tommy can't believe it's open until he gets to the coffin and sees that Ken Hilton is wearing a Maison Margiela mask made out of a profusion of glistening diamonds.

Instead of a rosary, there is a mirror clasped in Ken Hilton's hands. Tommy looks down at him and says a little prayer.

"Dear . . . um, dear God. I didn't mean for Ken Hilton to die. I just want my high school to be a happy place where people aren't afraid of coming to class because they spent less than a thousand dollars on their outfit. Is that such a sin?"

Back in the pew, Tommy watches his classmates line up to pay their respects.

When it's his turn, Ken Roberts inverted-crosses himself. "Dear Baphomet. I know I always prayed for Ken Hilton to just die already, but I didn't mean for him to get all of this attention for it. I guess I should've been praying for him to be forgotten. Is there a Block and Delete prayer I can recite?"

Ken Carson goes next. "Dear Baphomet, bruh. Please let Ken Hilton into hell even though he said your girl Beyoncé has the brain of a cognitively delayed fourth-grader and that's why she never gives interviews."

Todd stares down at Ken Hilton's corpse and wonders what his mom is cooking for dinner.

Brad Curtis chews the body of Christ with his mouth open. Crumbs fall into the casket. "Aw, man. I was praying to get stiff for Ken Hilton. Not for Ken Hilton to go stiff!"

Francie Fairchild twirls a strand of hair around her finger. "Dear Lord. Please forgive me and Brad for making Ken Hilton kill himself. And, um, now that he's dead—can I be prom Queen?"

It's like Ken Hilton was a fantasy all along. He stopped existing when Tommy stopped believing in him.

As soon as the service is over, Blaine makes a quick get-away. Tommy catches a glimpse of him driving off on his motorcycle. He hadn't even wanted to come to the funeral, but Tommy convinced him it would look weird if he didn't. Most of Willows High was going to be there, and the whole church would be counting Kens. Ken Carson and Ken Roberts sure anticipated fanfare—they arrived together in a limo.

Tommy walks through the cemetery, stopping next to the mound of dirt where Ken Hilton is going to spend eternity. He gazes across the tombstones, remembering the night he cast his wish to be a Ken.

"Ken Hilton's final box," a voice says behind him.

A startled Tommy almost falls into the grave. Allan takes his arm to steady him.

"I'm surprised you came," Tommy says.

"Thought I should." Allan shrugs. "We got the day off school for it."

"And you even wore pink."

The pants hem on Allan's suit is painfully too short, revealing a pair of pink socks.

"Didn't that funeral feel like a segment on *Entertainment Tonight*?" Allan asks. "When Father Dude took a selfie with

Ken Hilton's corpse I thought we were all going to burst into flames."

Tutti waves them over from the parking lot. She dyed her hair pink in remembrance.

"She's my ride," Allan says. "My car's in the shop. Not sure if it's going to pull through."

"The real tragedy of the day," Tommy jokes. They start walking back to the parking lot.

"You want a ride?" Tutti asks as they approach.

"I think I'll stick around for a bit," Tommy says. He wants to stay awhile because he can't quite grasp that Ken Hilton is really dead. Plastic is supposed to be permanent. Tommy wants to make sure Ken Hilton doesn't spring back to life and bring his revenge upon Willows.

Inside the church, Tommy finds Ken Roberts filling a douche with holy water.

"Hey, Ken," Ken Roberts says, placing the douche in his bag.

"I'm not a Ken," Tommy says.

Ken Roberts ignores him. "Hey, what do you think of Brad?"

"He's all right, I guess. Do you think he and Francie are going to get back together now that Ken has kicked it?"

"Ken Hilton and I were supposed to go on a double date with Brad and Todd this weekend," Ken Roberts says, "but the bih died on me."

"You and Todd?"

"He's had every girl at Willows High so he's finally moving on to me. Why don't you take Ken Hilton's place? Brad said he's into you."

"He did?" Tommy tries not to be flattered, but he can't help it. Brad's the most popular guy at school, after the Kens. "I don't know, I kind of have a thing going with Blaine . . ."

"Don't tell me you're monogamous? What *did* Ken Hilton ever see in you?"

"Why don't you ask Ken Carson to double?"

"He won't date Brad or any of the jocks. He's worried it'll come between their pre-game circle jerks. Oh, come on." Ken Roberts bounces up and down. "Todd won't go without Brad, and I'm dying for some varsity D!"

Before Tommy can say no again, they're interrupted by the sound of sobs coming down the aisle. They turn their heads, expecting to see Father Dude chastising one of the choirboys for using his teeth, but it's just Ken Hilton's mom, kneeling beside her son's casket. Her tears are brown from so much bronzer. They drip off her chin as she lifts her veil to kiss Ken Hilton's forehead. "Bye Felicia," she says.

Barbie comes down the aisle and air kisses both Ken Roberts and Tommy.

"Oh hai, gurs, hai. I'm heading to the after-party but I want to give you something first, Ken. Ken would've wanted you to have it." Barbie pulls the pink-rhinestone iPhone from her purse.

Ken Roberts grabs it with trembling hands. "I seriously *can't*. You're giving me *the* phone?"

Barbie dabs her teary filler with a tissue.

"He always said you were the second-bestseller."

Ken Carson looks down at his phone while driving his pink Jeep. Ken Roberts just *has* to text and gloat that he's the one who inherited Ken Hilton's pink-rhinestone iPhone.

Another text comes in, this time from Barbara Hilton, begging Ken Carson to come over. Barbie is the only safe pussy in Willows for him to tap.

Just about any girl at Willows High would let Ken Carson go down on them. He's Sport Superstar Ken. They line up.

But, like, no one can suspect he prefers pussy. A Ken hails dick alone. The most he can get away with is pretending he thinks eating out is fun, so the girls take it as a game.

There have been rare times he's gotten lucky at a party and gotten a BJ from a girl, but only if Ken Hilton was already overdosed. Ken Carson would never risk getting caught and discontinued.

It isn't always easy being a Ken. Being a lie. He has to keep a bigger lie box than Anaïs Nin! One of Ken Carson's secrets is that he reads more than celebrity blogs and tabloids. He hides books in his room like most kids hide drugs from their parents. Ken Hilton allowed but one kind of reading.

Whenever Ken Carson wants to read a book, he takes out his contacts because they're so annoying. He can't focus on the page. It's the strangest thing . . . it's like he can't read with them in. Not only because they blur the page, but also because he just can't seem to concentrate when he's wearing them. And if he does somehow manage to focus enough to read a paragraph, he doesn't really understand what he's reading. As soon as the contacts are in, Ken Carson can't read more than 280 characters.

Now that Ken Hilton's six feet under, maybe Ken Carson can reinvent the wheel. He can produce a Ken of the future and test it on the market. A Ken with brown eyes who is into girls. Ken: Straight Edition. But in today's market, will anyone buy it?

Heterosexuality is so last season.

Barbie's texts become increasingly hysterical. Ken Carson is sure she's downing a drink before sending each one. She FaceTimes him, smudged mascara rings around her teary eyes. Dr. Hilton went right back into surgery after Ken Hilton's funeral, and Barbie can't bear to be alone.

Since Ken Carson can't exactly nail any of the girls at school without being outed as straight and therefore a pseudo-Ken, he started seeing Barbie. She doesn't want anyone to know about their hookups either; the life her husband has her accustomed to depends on it.

They started hooking up one night when Ken Carson was sleeping over at Ken Hilton's house. Ken Carson woke up in the middle of the night to take a leak, and then snuck down to the kitchen to grab something to eat. That was yet another one of Ken Carson's secrets. He's a bad, bad Ken. He has an appetite.

Ken Carson made himself a baloney sandwich, and when he closed the fridge, Barbie was standing at the doorway in lace Frederick's of Hollywood.

"You have no idea how wet I am right now," she said. Ken Carson dropped his sandwich. It balanced on his hard dick sticking out of his plaid boxers. Barbie picked it up and took a bite.

That first time, he did her right there on the kitchen floor. He shoved the sandwich in her mouth to muffle her moans, but he wasn't actually worried about Ken Hilton waking up. Ken Hilton slept like he was turned off at night.

Ken Carson pulls through the gate, looking up at Ken Hilton's bedroom window as he parks. *Ken Hilton is dead.* Dude, what a great day!

Barbie is all over him as soon as he walks through the front door.

"I can't believe my baby's gone," she cries, pouring a glass of vodka and passing it to Ken Carson. She swigs straight from the bottle of Grey Goose.

"Is it true, Barbie?" Ken Carson asks. "Did you really give Ken Roberts Ken Hilton's phone?"

"Those two have been best friends since the second grade when they got caught stealing candy from Cartier. You just don't understand what sharing a police report does for a friendship."

"Ken Hilton hated Ken Roberts! He wished out loud for his bulimia to give him heart failure."

"All friendships have their ups and downs."

"After everything we've been through?" Ken Carson asks. "I feel all betrayed and shit."

"Oh, baby, don't say that." Barbie pets Ken Carson's face.

"I mean it, Barbie. It really, like, hurts."

"Here." Barbie digs through her Birkin and passes Ken Carson a bottle of pills. "Take something for the pain."

Ken Carson swallows a pill with a swig of vodka. He needs to be drunk to look at Barbie when they're going at it. *Pull it don't stuff it* is her Instagram bio.

"You're all I have left," Barbie says, grabbing Ken Carson's crotch through his pants. "You're like a son to me." She gives him a sloppy kiss, saliva stringing between their mouths. "Never leave me," she whimpers.

Ken Carson gets worried because Barbie lets the vodka bottle drop to the floor and throws her arms around his neck like she might want to *make love* to him, which is what she calls it sometimes when she's taken too many downers.

Thank Baphomet, dude, Barbie passes out on his chest. He pushes her off of him and onto the floor.

Ken Carson leaves with the bottle of vodka and gets back in his Jeep, touching up his hair in the rearview mirror. Dreamhouse is going to be lit!

On the drive, he starts to get sleepy. What was that pill Barbie gave him? He opens the glove compartment and digs around for some blow. After a couple sniffs straight from the bag, he's awake.

He's living.

DATE NIGHT AND ACCESSORIES PLAYSET

In the days following Ken Hilton's funeral, the students of Willows High have to face the reality of his death. The queen has been slain. And they need someone to blame.

The teardown of Brad Curtis is *so* much fun!

Brad is the victim of merciless attacks in the comments section of SoFamous, and bumped from the center table at the caf. One of Ken Roberts's first moves as queen regent is to excommunicate him. Ken Roberts isn't exactly bummed that Ken Hilton is dead, but it would be bad for his image if that were popular knowledge. Brad has to be sacrificed. He's blacklisted everywhere—turned away at the door of Dreamhouse, and even benched by Coach Summers during a Barks game.

The court of public opinion has ruled that Ken Hilton was driven to suicide because his quarterback boyfriend couldn't get it up. Brad was never really into Ken Hilton; he was a social climber using Ken Hilton for fame while still harboring feelings for his ex.

Francie Fairchild is the other woman, but that only increases her popularity. When Ken Hilton stole her boyfriend, everyone thought she was totally over. She'd been the most popular girl at school one day, and unfollowed by everyone the next. But now that it's been revealed that she and Brad never really broke things off, and that Francie was the only person Ken Hilton was jealous of, her stats are skyrocketing.

If Brad couldn't get it up for Ken Hilton, something must be wrong with him. And he calls himself a jock? A post-op tranny could still manage to get it up for Ken Hilton—that's how hot he was.

Ken Roberts posts about Brad and Ken Hilton's faux-mance on SoFamous. Without Ken Hilton dominating him, he no longer feels the urge to purge—except all of Ken Hilton's secrets.

Evidently, Ken Hilton wasn't so perfect after all. He had one testicle that was bigger than the other, Harvey Weinstein never invited him up to a hotel room to talk about a movie role (despite Ken Hilton's Twitter claims to the contrary), and he wasn't a natural blond. When Ken Roberts posts a photo of Ken Hilton with roots, everyone knows Ken Hilton must be rolling in his grave. #ginger. Willows High isn't pre-pared for the shock. Ken Hilton was a fire-crotch! If the truth had come out while he was alive, he would've been forgotten at the bottom of the toy box.

Tommy is grateful for the distractions. He keeps an eye on SoFamous, but there's nothing that links him or Blaine to Ken Hilton's death—just endless posts exposing the real Ken Hilton, and shading Brad.

Brad copes with the pressure of fame by hitting the bot-tle hard. Ken Roberts texts Tommy before their double date to tell him that Brad called him, slurring his words and saying he hopes Tommy will help put him back in the shopping cart.

"His sales are, like, way down," Ken Roberts says. "But if he can bag another Ken . . ."

Tommy didn't exactly consent to the double date, but Ken Roberts doesn't take no for an answer. The weekend comes around and Brad pulls up to Tommy's house in his red Mustang with Ken Roberts and Todd in the backseat. They're all wasted.

Ken Roberts's hand is already in Todd's pants, and Todd is taking shots from a bottle of Jack Daniel's to get to the level where he's okay with it.

The Mustang swerves as they drive to The Hills. Brad is obviously seeing double. Tommy buckles in.

"Maybe I should drive," he suggests. Brad brushes him off and the car swerves. Tommy looks down at his phone to distract himself from his impending death. Still no text from Blaine. Tommy casually mentioned that he was going on the double date to see if it would make Blaine jealous. He may not be a Ken anymore, but he learned a thing or two during his brief tenure.

Brad lurches to a stop at the peak. The Mustang almost rolls right over.

"Kens' Trail," Tommy says. "How romantic." The hiker's path has been unofficially named after the Kens because it's where they usually end up with their dates.

Todd anxiously finishes the bottle of JD before stepping out.

They've barely made it a few feet down the trail before Ken Roberts grabs Todd by his varsity jacket and pulls him behind a tree.

Brad and Tommy share an awkward glance. Tommy has his hands in the pockets of his jeans. Brad pulls out a flask and takes a generous sip.

When he suddenly steps closer to Tommy and kisses him, Tommy's too surprised to react. He feels Brad's tongue jamming into his mouth urgently, like he's trying to prove that he really is a stud, the ultimate jock pig, conqueror of Ken. It doesn't feel right, but Tommy gives in and kisses him back. He imagines he's kissing Blaine. They pull apart and Tommy sees Brad's eyes, lit up by stars, fall to the path with shame.

"Nothing?"

"I just drank too much," Brad says defensively. "Just give me a minute."

"It's okay," Tommy says. "I don't mind."

They hear Ken Roberts moaning behind the bushes and Brad gets even more anxious, like he's worried Todd is going to get promoted on the Barks or something.

"Let's try again." He grabs Tommy and slobbers all over him.

"Ew, 'zif!" Tommy pushes him away. Brad falls onto the path and doesn't get back up. He's out cold.

There's a rumbling above and Tommy blinks through a light shining from the peak. He follows the light back down the trail and, coming out in the clearing, finds Blaine idling on his motorcycle. *Madly* jealous, obviously. Tommy smiles and quickly jumps on the back of the bike.

"How'd you know where to find me?" he asks.

Blaine revs the engine.

"Ken Roberts checks in *everywhere*."

"It's really coming along." Tommy climbs over the chain-link fence and looks up at the mall. The cement has been laid in the parking lot, and the windows have all been fitted with glass. A PLASTIC PLACE marquee protrudes above the entrance with the same lettering as the WILLOWSLAND sign.

"Grand opening in a few weeks," Blaine says.

The mall is locked down, but Blaine knows a way in through a basement side door. "I thought you'd appreciate the attention to detail." He shows Tommy how the pipes have all been freshly painted pink.

"Your dad sure has found the spirit of Willows . . . He's pretty influenced by the Kens, huh?"

"Artificiality is critique." Blaine shrugs. Tommy can't tell if Blaine knows about Ken Roberts and his dad or not.

They walk down the dark basement hallway. Tommy looks over at Blaine.

"You really rescued me tonight. I shouldn't have even gone. Brad's just trying to use me to restore his popularity."

"I wanted to see for myself," Blaine says. "The Kens haven't lost their stronghold, have they?"

"It's like they're stronger than ever. Like *we* made them stronger than ever."

"I was afraid of that."

Tommy isn't expecting it when Blaine pushes him against the wall and kisses him.

It isn't like kissing Brad at all. It isn't wet and it doesn't taste like Taco Accessory and whiskey. It's short and sweet; Tommy barely has time to close his eyes. But it's good. So good it makes him feel like a Ken again. Breathless.

"What was that for?" Tommy's glad it's dark in the basement so Blaine can't see how big his, um, smile is.

"Just wanted to see what all the fuss was about," Blaine says.

"It didn't mean anything tonight with Brad. Just so you know."

"Nothing means anything."

"I just thought that maybe you—"

"Aw." Blaine pats Tommy's head. "Look at you, thinking and stuff."

TEEN TALK

They're staring as he makes his way to his locker.

A group of Barks players point and laugh. Cold sweat coats his body. They know. He's sure of it. Everyone knows!

Tommy pulls out his phone and attempts to load SoFamous. He's trying not to panic, but he feels like the box is closing in on him.

SoFamous won't load, but something is definitely up. Francie and Midge pass him, cheer skirts swaying from side to side so sharply they could cut a bitch. They cling to each other's arms, looking him up and down and whispering to each other.

Tommy walks down the hall, lifting his phone above his head to try to find a connection. He bumps into a trash bin and notices Allan in the science lab with Mr. Hadley, standing at the doorway of the supplies closet. Allan helps out in the lab for extra credit.

"Very distressing." Mr. Hadley rubs his chin. "Very distressing indeed."

"What's going on?" Tommy asks as he enters.

"Someone broke into the supplies closet." Allan looks back at him. "We're missing sulfuric acid and nitric acid."

"I'll have to report this to Principal Elliot at once," Mr. Hadley says. "I shudder to think of the ways in which corrosive substances might be used in today's world . . ."

Mr. Hadley leaves the class, muttering to himself.

"Think it's serious?" Tommy asks.

"Mr. Hadley probably misplaced an order or something. He's a mad scientist, always in his head. One day he came to school without any pants on."

"Oh yeah." Tommy remembers. "He was Ken Hilton's favorite teacher."

A group of kids in the hallway passes the lab door. They see Tommy and stop to take a photo of him.

"Do you know what's going on?" Tommy asks Allan. He checks his phone to see if SoFamous will load. Still nothing.

"Is it true?" Allan says quietly. "About you and Brad?"

"What about me and Brad?"

"Did you guys really go on a date this weekend?"

"I wouldn't really call it a date. I left halfway through."

"Well, that's not what he's saying."

Tommy waits for him to go on, watching as Allan fidgets uncomfortably.

"He's saying that you guys went all the way and that you're"—Allan spits the last part out as fast as he can—"a messy bottom."

"A *what*?" Tommy gasps.

"So it isn't true?"

"Of course it isn't true! He's just trying to save face and

restore his I-stick-it-in-anything jock image because everyone knows he couldn't satisfy Ken Hilton!"

For the rest of the day, Tommy has all eyes and lenses on
him. Someone even puts a whoopee cushion on his seat in
math class. Tommy doesn't get off on the fact that he's
bumped Ken Hilton from the top trending story on
SoFamous. His skin just isn't thick enough plastic to deal
with the scrutiny.

He escapes to Blaine's house after school. They sit on the
couch and Blaine turns on the TV. *Willows News* comes on.
Stacie Skipper is doing a segment on pre-teen boob jobs.

Blaine's dad gets home from work, and Tommy sits up a
little straighter. He's glad his face is still frozen with Botox,
because if it weren't he's sure Blaine's dad would be able to
tell that Tommy knows his dirty secret . . . But Scott Gordon
barely registers Tommy as he barrels into the living room,
loosening his red tie and shouting at the top of his lungs.

"Goddamn terrorists!"

"Hard day at work, Pops?" Blaine asks without averting
his eyes from the TV.

"Some Twitter tribe of hairy-armpit bitches have started
a petition to stop me from opening Plastic Place. They want
to turn the building into a mosque. A fucking mosque! All
because Willows was voted the least diverse city in America.
Fucking SJWs."

Tommy whispers to Blaine. "SJWs?"

"Social justice warriors," he says.

Scott looks at Tommy for the first time. He jumps back.

"Ken?" he chokes.

"You look like you've seen a ghost." Blaine laughs at his dad. "Looks like the kid on the news who killed himself, right? But this is my friend Tommy."

"Nice to meet you, sir." Tommy puts out his hand for Blaine's dad to shake. Scott offers a fist-bump instead.

"Major germophobe," Blaine explains under his breath.

Scott stares at Tommy for another beat, then continues ranting. "You'd think they'd be grateful. Plastic Place will be the biggest building in Willows!"

"Bigger than the one mom bungee-jumped off of in Ohio?" Blaine asks. "Too bad she forgot the cord, huh Pops?"

Blaine's dad just stares at him. Tommy shifts on the couch uncomfortably.

"You kids skedaddle." Scott grabs the remote. "I need to Wii Fit and blow off some steam."

———

"How much do you want to bet that Twitter petition to stop Plastic Place is being signed by people who don't even live in Willows?" Blaine asks up in his room. "No one in this town cares about anything but their latest selfie."

They sit on Blaine's bed. Tommy glances over at Blaine

scrolling through his phone and wonders if they're going to kiss again.

Blaine flashes Tommy Brad's latest Instagram photo of him holding two male blow-up dolls. The caption says, "2 Kens Down, 2 to Go." It's been Liked more than five hundred times.

"Another Ken product." Blaine exits out of the screen.

"It's such a Ken Hilton move," Tommy says. "They really were perfect for each other."

"Brad Curtis has to be brought down."

"He's not worth the effort. Besides, he's the only black kid at Willows High. Who can blame him for being so insecure?"

"You're just going to give him a pass for making up that lie about you?"

"What would you suggest, another pill bomb?"

Blaine jumps off the bed and starts pacing.

"I was joking," Tommy says nervously.

"Willows is the least diverse city in America . . . Brad Curtis is the only black kid at Willows High . . ." A familiar light appears in Blaine's eyes. "Was that Brad's Mustang parked on the peak?"

OREO BARBIE

Brad Curtis's baby is the red Mustang his father gave him for his sixteenth birthday. He had a Hot Wheel just like it as a kid; it was his favorite toy to play with. Brad loves to drive. With the road wide open in front of him he doesn't have to worry about any of the usual things that weigh heavily on him—football stats, what to eat next, how long he can keep stealing his dad's Viagra without him noticing.

He started popping the pills whenever he had a date with Ken Hilton, but when Ken Hilton found out he was more insulted than ever. "*I'm* supposed to be your drug," he pouted. Brad started getting wasted every time they were together so that he could have something to blame for his impotence. He was terrified of losing his ticket to the top. Dating Ken Hilton was the best thing that had ever happened to him. He'd always been popular, but once he started dating a Ken, *the* Ken, he got so many new followers that Dippity-Do was sending him DMs and paying him to promote their products. Going gay for Ken Hilton made him a star, and there was no way he was going back to being basic, even if it meant he had to give up his first love, Francie Fairchild—the finest piece of ass in Willows.

Word on SoFamous is that Francie is hooking up with Todd, and it kills him, but no way is Brad taking her back even now that Ken Hilton is dead. His status is more vulnerable than ever. He has to rebound.

After dating a Ken there's nowhere to go but down, unless, of course, he dates another Ken. That had been the plan with Ken Rawlins, but things hadn't gone as he'd hoped. But Brad still managed to use him . . .

The rumor he started about their date is helping buff up his stats. He may be a master at the Kens' game, but Brad does feel slightly bad for his lie. There was just no way around it. Ken Hilton was the one who taught him that the *pop* in *popularity* stands for popping off a bitch's head to get ahead. He did what he had to do. Now, to really secure his position at Willows High, he's going to ask Ken Roberts out to Dreamhouse.

Dating a Ken isn't easy. For someone who once wrote a post on SoFamous promoting a diet of one-day-on-one-day-off eating, Ken Hilton sure had a sweet tooth. But he'd only eat pink candies. Pink jellybeans, pink Starbursts, pink gummies . . . pink, pink, pink! Coach Summers noticed Brad had put on an extra layer. He couldn't help it. He had to eat the offending junk before Ken Hilton had a meltdown.

But the sacrifices are worth it for the glory. Brad wakes up in the morning and gets ready for an early football practice singing "I Just Can't Wait to Be King."

Brad's Mustang sparkles in the driveway.

Parked on the other side of the road from Brad's house, out of sight, is Blaine's motorcycle. Blaine and Tommy sneak onto Brad's property, ducking behind his Mustang. Blaine puts the sleeve of his leather jacket over his fist and punches out one of the taillights. Broken glass falls to the cement.

They retreat back to the bike, where they have a view of Brad's front door through the shrubs. Brad comes out, whistling to himself. He tosses his keys in the air and catches them in the palm of his hand. As he pulls out onto the street, he doesn't notice the Harley trailing him at a distance.

A few blocks in, Blaine pulls his bike over to the side of the road and makes a call to the Willows Police Department.

"Yes, Officer," he says, "there's an erratic driver on Hillcrest Road, weaving between the lines. He's driving a red Mustang, and the left taillight is broken. Did I get a look at him?" Blaine winks at Tommy. "Why yes, I did, Officer. He appears to be a young African-American male."

Police sirens are immediately heard in the distance.

"This is so wrong," Tommy says, "but so ingenious! If I didn't totally hate Brad I'd feel bad for him. Just think how crushed he's going to be when we post a video of the King of Willows High being taken down a peg by one of the Willows' finest. No one will ever respect him again if we can catch him being submissive to someone who works for the *government*!"

A WPD cruiser soars by. Blaine pulls up behind it, staying

far enough back so that they're carefully concealed by the curve of the corner. Tommy and Blaine watch as the Mustang is pulled over. Blaine hits Record on his phone.

A police officer steps out of the cruiser, pulling out his Glock 22 before he's even approached the vehicle.

Tommy and Blaine are close enough to hear the conversation.

"Is there a problem, Officer?" Brad asks, unrolling his window.

The officer screams, "Put your hands up!"

Brad's seen enough YouTube videos to know to do as he's told. He lifts his hands in the air.

"I'm sorry if I was speeding, sir. I'm on my way to football practice and Coach hates it when we're late."

"Do you have license and registration for this vehicle?"

"Yes, sir." Brad lowers his hands to reach for the glove compartment and pull out the registration.

Before Brad can reach over, the officer shoots him point-blank ten times.

"I said put your hands up!" the officer shouts as he keeps shooting. Finally, he puts away his gun and takes off his aviator glasses, wiping a speck of blood from the lens. He calls in the shooting. "Suspect appeared to be reaching for a firearm," he tells the dispatcher.

Tommy opens his mouth to scream but no sound comes out. He wants to jump off the back of Blaine's motorcycle and charge at the officer, to bash his head into the road over and over. But Blaine's bike is roaring to life and they're speeding in the opposite direction.

"He killed him!" Tommy jumps off the back of the motor-cycle as soon as it comes to a stop in the parking lot of Willows High. "I lost track of how many times he shot him!"

"Ten," Blaine says. "He just kept going and going!"

Tommy bends over, holding onto his knees and trying to catch his breath.

"This wasn't supposed to happen," he says. "This wasn't supposed to happen."

"Think of it this way: at least we won't have to write a suicide post this time."

"You sound like you expected this." Tommy forces himself erect. He's shaking.

"Don't be ridiculous." Blaine looks away. "How could I have known?"

"It was just supposed to be a prank," Tommy says. "A video that made Brad, not me, the laughingstock of Willows High. But now he's dead! Oh God. He's dead. And it's all my fault."

"You can't take credit for the racist climate in this country, Tommy. You're not *that* good."

"How can you be so cool about this?"

Tommy usually finds Blaine's nonchalance sexy. Blaine's bad, and that's why Tommy wants him so badly. But this time it just scares him.

Blaine reaches into the pocket of his jacket for his phone.

"What are you doing?" Tommy asks.

"Anonymously submitting the video of the shooting to SoFamous. Think there'll be any riots?"

Tommy runs his hands through his hair, pulling on his blond. The scream he's been holding inside is finally released.

Blaine arches an eyebrow at him over the top of his phone. "Guilt is a useless emotion. There isn't even an emoji for it."

"I just wanted to humiliate him . . ."

"If it wasn't a broken taillight, it would've been a turn signal that some copper pretended he didn't see."

"We can turn ourselves in. The cop will spin things to make it seem like Brad was in the wrong, but we can explain that Brad was totally innocent. It's the least we can do for him."

"You can't bring him back, Tommy."

"I'm not trying to bring him back! I'm trying to bring *myself* back."

"You'll have to book another appointment with Dr. Hilton for that."

Tommy lunges at Blaine. They throw down in the middle of the parking lot. Tommy gets in a few punches, but Blaine has him pinned fast. They're both breathing heavily as Blaine stares down into Tommy's eyes.

"Time to pretend it's just another perfect day in perfect Willows," he says.

SPARKLE SURPRISE

Just like Ken Hilton, Brad is even more popular in death.

Ken Roberts stands in the middle of the hallway of Willows High, fake-sobbing. "I can't believe it. I just can't believe it!"

Everyone is surprised because Kens usually reserve that level of emotion for Comme des Garçons. They didn't realize Ken Roberts and Brad were that close. They weren't. Ken Roberts is just freaking out because one of the pink rhinestones on Ken Hilton's old iPhone fell off.

Francie and the cheer squad are huddled together down the hall. Francie is milking a second wave of popularity. First she was the reason Ken Hilton killed himself, and now she's lost Brad, the love of her life—or at least of her Facebook timeline. The sympathy Likes are staggering.

Tommy walks down the hall with his head bowed. Well, he got what he wanted. No one is talking about his date with Brad anymore. The most-trending post on SoFamous is the video of Brad being shot.

"Why so serious, Ken?" Ken Roberts, standing with Ken Carson, stops Tommy.

"Yeah, dude." Ken Carson flips his hair. "It's not like someone's Instagram account got suspended."

Ken Roberts lifts his shirt. "#freethenipple."

"For the last time, I am *not* a Ken. Aren't you guys the least bit sad that Brad's dead?"

"It's, like, so convenient," Ken Roberts says. "I was wondering where to pre-game before my coronation party this weekend. And now it's, like, duh! We can pre-game at Famous Family for Brad's funeral. Churches are *stocked* with wine."

"Coronation party?"

Ken Roberts bobbles. "Party dresses are fun!"

Famous Family is even more packed for Brad's funeral than it was for Ken Hilton's. Everyone who missed the first major social event of the season lines up outside the church doors all night for a seat to the second coming.

Father Dude takes to the podium in blackface.

"Brad Curtis is dead," he begins his sermon, "and I blame the Oscars."

Tommy zones out after that. He's staring at Brad's family in the front pew. Brad's little brother is crying. Tommy closes his eyes and hears bullets in his head. As if he can sense Tommy is about to blow, Blaine takes his hand and gives it a squeeze. A little too tightly.

Ken Roberts's party is at his house directly following the funeral. Everyone is wine drunk and totally feels like their parents. Tommy gets even drunker than he was at Dreamhouse. He's afraid he'll never be able to get the image of Brad being shot out of his head.

The light fixture in the middle of the living room ceiling has been replaced by a giant disco ball almost as shiny as the vintage Bob Mackie ensemble Ken Roberts is wearing, complete with a tiara.

Ken Roberts is floating on a giant inflatable unicorn in the pool, being pushed around by the Barks players.

The whole school is at the party. Tommy even spots Allan and Tutti in the crowd. They find him under the disco ball.

"Tutti dragged me," Allan says. "She said we were going to a protest. I should've known."

Tommy grabs a red plastic cup out of someone's hand and chugs from it. It's vodka and he hates the taste, but he doesn't care. He pretends not to notice Allan and Tutti share a look.

"You okay?" Tutti asks.

"Yes, sir," Tommy says.

The music fades and the Barks glide Ken Roberts's unicorn to the edge of the pool. Ken Carson lifts Ken Roberts off the floating device. Midge passes him a microphone.

"Welcome to my realm, bitches," Ken Roberts screams.

The partyers lift their cups and cheer.

"As your queen, I fully expect you to bend the knee," Ken Roberts says. "And if you're lucky, I'll bend the knee for you!" He tickles Todd's bare, wet chest before turning back to his people. "Now, a few rules of my reign. From now on, all common students must pay me a cut of their lunch money or

I won't just chop off your head, I'll chop off your followers! Also, no one can sit at their desks or table in the caf until I've taken my seat, and, like, you have to wait to eat your lunch until I've finished mine. Oh, and . . ."

Allan snorts. "Is he serious?"

"At least he's not bulimic anymore and will only be eating one helping," Tutti says.

"Now let's party!" Ken Roberts yells over the cheering crowd. The music goes back up and he starts dancing on a lounge chair.

Tommy drops his red plastic cup to the floor.

"I have to find Blaine," he says, pushing his way through the crowd.

Tommy really thought that without Ken Hilton terrorizing the halls of Willows High, school would change. Was he totally wrong to think there was something sweet about Ken Roberts? He seemed so insecure, puking up his feelings. Ken Hilton pushed Ken Roberts down, and Tommy thought that if Ken Hilton was out of the picture, Ken Roberts might finally find the strength to become his own person. He should've known he'd find the strength to become Ken Hilton.

Tommy looks through the house, finally finding Blaine in Ken Roberts's bedroom, which is modeled after Marie Antoinette's bedroom in the Sofia Coppola movie. The lights are off. On top of a vanity is the pink-rhinestone iPhone Ken Roberts inherited from Ken Hilton. It glows in the dark.

The hallway light spills into the room and cuts across Blaine's face, leaving half of him in shadow. "This thing's more cursed than the Hope Diamond." He points at the phone.

Music fades as Tommy shuts the bedroom door and leans against it. He tries to stop the room from spinning by closing his eyes. "It's never going to end, is it?" he asks.

"The crown may be on a new head, but the head thinks the same," Blaine says. "That is to say, not at all. It's *Animal Farm*. The pigs are wearing designer."

Tommy stumbles through the darkness over to Blaine, clinging to the arm of his leather jacket. "Why don't we leave Willows?" he slurs. "Let's take your bike and go! Away from the Kens . . . Somewhere over the plastic, where the Kens haven't made being gay trendy. It'll be like the olden days. Kind of romantic, when you think about it."

Blaine pulls his arm away, leaving Tommy swaying.

"Running isn't an option. We have two choices: live or let die."

Tommy falls back on Ken Roberts's canopy bed. His eyelids are drooping.

"Ken Roberts posted a photo earlier of that tiara he's wearing in a Cartier box," Blaine says. "Maybe we've been thinking too small. We need to cut off their supplier . . . Who funds the Kens?"

Tommy puts a hand to his clammy forehead. "You really don't know, do you?"

"Know what?"

"Who do you think came up with a name like Plastic Place?" Tommy murmurs. "Ken Roberts is on your dad's payroll." He closes his eyes and fades out. "Duh."

The party is over when Tommy comes to. His head is pounding and his throat is dry. He doesn't know why he's in Ken Roberts's room. The last thing he remembers is a unicorn and parts of Ken Roberts's speech. Everything after that is blank.

Tommy climbs off the bed and stumbles his way out into the hall. The house is empty. It has the eerie silence of an after-party's last breath—a static coming from somewhere, in the floor maybe, buried underneath red plastic cups and glitter. Lights are flickering down the hallway. Tommy edges his way along the wall.

Myriad spots of light spin around the living room.

Ken Roberts is straddling the disco ball, going around and around with each rotation. There's a bottle of champagne tucked under his arm. He takes a sip and the bottle slips out of his hand, smashing to the floor. Ken Roberts doesn't even notice.

Plaster sprinkles down on his tiara.

The ceiling cracks around the pole that holds up the disco ball. A chunk of roof comes down, landing on Ken Roberts's head and knocking him unconscious to the floor. The disco ball falls after him. Thousands of mirrored facets explode everywhere.

Tommy approaches slowly, the disco debris crunching under his feet.

Not again . . .

"Ken?" he whispers.

PART 4

RECALL

"Don't dwell on what happened, no matter how bad it was. Find something else to do. Find something to do to help others."

RUTH HANDLER

HAUNTED BEAUTY GHOST

Everyone's hung over the day after Brad's funeral and Ken Roberts's epic party. Thankfully, classes are canceled. Principal Elliot calls an assembly to help the students of Willows High cope with the murder. He opens the gym floor to anyone who wants to share their feelings, and keeps saying "trigger warning," which is maybe a manufacturing error.

Tommy is sitting between Allan and Blaine.

"Where's Tutti?" he asks Allan.

"Haven't seen her since this morning."

Principal Elliot is interrupted by Ken Roberts's late arrival. For a moment at the party, Tommy thought Ken Hilton 2.0 had dropped dead, beautiful. But Ken Roberts's eyes had flung open and Tommy jumped back. He snuck out of Ken Roberts's house, trying not to let himself feel disappointed.

Ken Roberts makes a grand entrance with Francie and Midge and the rest of his cheer squad trailing behind him. They strut right up to the middle of the bleachers, expecting everyone to shuffle over and make room for them.

"This is an open platform for anyone who needs it," Principal Elliot is saying. "Willows High has been devastated by yet another tragic loss, but we will not be defeated! Is there anyone who would like to say a few words?"

Francie Fairchild stands up. The gym goes still and quiet. Even Ken Roberts is surprisingly respectful. He doesn't pull out his phone to check Grindr until Francie has already started speaking.

"I just want to say the fight is real," Francie says. "And, like, at winter formal when I had cornrows and everyone said I was appropriating black culture I was really offended because it's, like, I'm black inside. Well, I've had black *inside* of me . . ."

Francie wipes away a tear that isn't coming.

"We love you, Francie," Todd yells from the bleachers.

Tommy can't take it anymore. He gets up and storms out of the gym.

"Sometimes the grief is just too much to take," Principal Elliot calls after him.

He glides down the empty hall, his eyes wide open but not really seeing anything, like Ken Roberts when he regained consciousness after falling off the disco ball.

At his locker he automatically puts in the combination. He still has a bottle of the pain meds Dr. Hilton prescribed after his surgeries.

In the bathroom, Tommy turns on the tap and throws some water on his face. When he looks up into the mirror, his old face is reflected back at him. He slowly raises his hand and touches the glass, jerking his hand away when his reflection is left with blood smeared across the cheek. He hits the glass, cracking it, to make the image disappear.

Tommy pulls the cap off the bottle and dumps the pills into the palm of his hand, shoving them in his mouth. But before he can swallow, the bathroom door swings open and Allan bursts in.

"Are you crazy?" He knocks the bottle out of Tommy's hand.

Pastel pretties scatter across the floor. Allan wraps his arm around Tommy's stomach and squeezes. Tommy coughs out pills into the sink.

"What's gotten into you? Please tell me you're not trying to kill yourself to stay on trend?"

"You don't understand." Tommy grips the sink. "I feel like it's my fault."

"What is?"

"All of it! Allan, I—"

They're interrupted by the door swinging open. Ken Roberts enters and looks around.

"So this is the boys' room," he says.

"Can I help you?" Allan asks.

Ken Roberts picks up a pill off the floor, blows on it and pops it in his mouth.

"I saw you two run off." He swallows effortlessly. "I assume you've heard?"

"Heard what?"

"There's been a suicide. Well, attempted."

Tommy's heart lodges in his throat. Another one? Who has Blaine killed now? And without him? That *bastard*!

"Who?" Allan asks.

"Two-Ton Tutti. She slit her wrist this morning."

"Tutti?" Allan looks at Tommy with disbelief.

"Is she okay?" Tommy asks.

"According to my sources she barely broke skin. Just another example of a loser trying to regram the cool kids."

Allan can barely contain himself. "You're a monster!" he screams.

"Yassss, Gaga. I just posted a scan of her suicide note on SoFamous. She wrote it in cursive! Can you believe that? No one can read it."

Ken Roberts looks at his freshly manicured claws. "Face it, Tutti started tweeting @SuicidePrevention from her crib. It was only a matter of time."

"I'm going to the hospital," Allan says.

"I'll come with you."

Ken Roberts blocks Tommy. "Not so fast. We need to talk."

Tommy glares at him. "Fine. Let's end this." He turns to Allan. "Tell Tutti I'm on my way?"

Allan glances at the pills in the sink.

"Are you sure you're going to be okay?"

"I promise." Tommy nods.

Ken Roberts nudges Tommy out of the way and takes over the mirror. A kaleidoscope of Kens is reflected in the cracked glass.

"You were a Ken and now you're hanging out with him again?" he asks as the door swings shut.

"I'd rather hang out with Allan than you any day."

"If I had feelings, they'd totally be hurt right now."

"What do you want, Ken?"

Ken Roberts pulls out a tube of lip gloss and touches up. He smacks his lips together.

"Ken Hilton made you his son of God, and then killed you off. Well, I'm God now. And it's time for your resurrection."

"I'm no longer deluded enough to want to be a Ken."

"You have to! Ken Carson has grown a conscience. It must be a defect."

"What do you mean?"

"Tutti's suicide attempt got to him. He thinks that just because she tried to kill herself we should stop being so mean."

"Perish the thought," Tommy says sarcastically.

"He just hasn't been doing enough coke lately."

"Why are you such a bitch?"

Ken Roberts holds up Ken Hilton's sparkling pink-rhinestone iPhone. "Because it's my divine right to rule."

"Some rulers get their heads chopped off."

"And some chop off everyone else's. Oh, come on, Thomas. I *need* you."

"Why?"

"I need a Ken on each side of my faces! I'm, like, giving you a second chance to be something here."

"Be nothing, you mean."

"Okay, so you're basic and don't know how to read. Big deal. Just shut up and look pretty. It's not that hard."

Tommy rolls his eyes. "Your reality check bounced."

They hear chanting coming from outside. "Fight! Fight! Fight!" Through the window they see a crowd gathering around Ken Carson and Todd, who are wrestling on the field.

"What's with those two?" Tommy asks.

"Ken Carson is defending Tutti's honor or some shit. I'm really thinking of returning him."

"Why are you so determined to follow Ken Hilton's path? You have a chance to do something different. Willows High would change if you were a kind ruler."

"What kind of ruler?"

"No, a kind ruler. As in good?"

Ken Roberts just blinks.

CURVY MODEL

Tutti is sitting up in her hospital bed completing a tabloid magazine crossword puzzle when Tommy enters carrying flowers. Yellow roses, definitely not pink.

"Killer countess who bathed in the blood of her servants for eternal youth?" Tutti asks. "Eleven letters."

"Lady Báthory," Tommy says. "Ken Hilton considered using it instead of Sandy Hooker as his drag name."

"Báthory." Tutti scribbles it in. "Thanks."

She folds up the magazine and Tommy passes her the bouquet. She takes it with a bandaged wrist.

"You didn't have to, but they're beautiful." She smells a rose. "You just missed Allan."

"Poor Allan. He's really going through it with us for friends."

"What have I missed now? If only I could PVR the halls of Willows High!"

Tommy pulls up a chair next to Tutti's bed.

"Why'd you do it, Toots? You didn't seem depressed. You're the most positive person I know."

"I didn't mean to actually kill myself. I didn't cut that deep. My parents overreacted, like I knew they would. I just thought that if it looked like I had tried . . . then maybe Ken Roberts would back off."

"What'd he do? I mean, what hasn't he done? But you never let the Kens get to you before."

"Because I thought Ken Hilton was the evil one, and Ken Roberts and Ken Carson weren't actually cruel, they were just his followers. I could deal with that. Ken Hilton was the villain, the one we loved to hate. But now Ken Roberts has taken his place and I don't love to hate him, I just plain hate him. He posted a photo of the vending machine to SoFamous and captioned it, 'Tutti's Locker.' During first period Todd passed me chocolate bars and said I forgot my books."

"So I guess that's why Ken Carson was fighting him," Tommy says.

"Ken Carson got in a fight with Todd over *me*?"

"He's the only Ken with a soul. Ken Roberts is the hollow one. I actually felt sorry for Ken Roberts while I was briefly a Ken. Ken Hilton reeled him in and then cast him off as he pleased. Ken Roberts was never allowed to keep his platforms firmly on the ground."

"Well, they are now," Tutti says. "And he's walking over everyone with them."

Tommy traces Tutti's bandage. "Something tells me Ken Roberts was built to self-destruct."

SHAVING FUN

The next morning, Tommy gets a text from Blaine telling him to come over before school.

When he arrives, the door to Blaine's house is partially open. It creaks as Tommy pushes it all the way open and steps into the dark foyer.

"Blaine?" Tommy calls.

A gust of wind slams the door shut behind him.

None of the lights on the main floor of the house are on, so Tommy climbs the stairs thinking Blaine must be in his bedroom. The lights are off upstairs too, except for one at the end of the hallway. Tommy walks toward it, coming to an abrupt stop in the middle of the hall when he sees the barrel of a gun poking around the corner of a doorway. He feels a jolt of fear and is about to dive out of the way but stops himself. He smiles and strikes a pose. The trigger clicks.

"Shit," he hears Blaine say. "I'm out of bullets."

Blaine places the gun on the counter next to the sink. Tommy finds him standing in the bathroom, his face lathered up with shaving gel. Blaine runs a razor under the tap.

"Does it have batteries or a charger?" Tommy asks. He leans against the counter and picks up the camera gun, weighing it in his hand. "Heavier than I thought it would be."

Tommy watches Blaine shaving in the reflection of the mirror. *What a hunk.*

"Why don't we skip school?" Tommy asks. "Maybe we could go for another skinny dip . . ."

They hear the sound of the front door opening and closing downstairs, followed by crackling laughter.

"Great." Tommy drops the camera gun. "The Donald's home."

Blaine's dad barrels up the stairs and pokes his head through the bathroom doorway.

"Stopped by the courthouse early this morning and . . . we beat the SJWs!" He gives Tommy and Blaine a thumbs-up. "Did I say I was going to build a mall?" He punches Blaine's arm. "I only wish I could find a way to make those terrorist-loving bitches pay for it."

Snap, Crackle, Scott walks off.

"Your father is *such* a bigot," Tommy says. "Talk about self-loathing," he adds under his breath.

The razor nicks Blaine's chin. He winces as he attempts to shave over it.

"Here, let me." Tommy takes the razor out of Blaine's hand and starts shaving for him.

"So how much of Ken Roberts's little coronation do you remember?" Blaine asks.

"Let's just say I woke up in Ken Roberts's bedroom and I have no idea how I got there."

"Yeah, you were pretty wasted."

"I guess so. I don't even remember seeing you." Tommy glides the razor down Blaine's jawline. "Drinking that night was the only way I could handle Ken Roberts. He's totally irredeemable. Did you hear about Tutti? Is that why you wanted me to come over?"

"So she followed the trend, huh? I wonder if there will be others."

"I don't think she really wanted to die."

"They always pretend they didn't want to die when they live. And when they do die, everyone else pretends they didn't want to die. After my mom nose-dived off the roof, everyone tried to act like it was a big accident. Like her wings just didn't flap."

Tommy holds the razor suspended in front of Blaine's cheek. He wishes he could think of something to say, but in the end he just finishes shaving and watches as Blaine rinses off. Blaine pats his face dry with a towel, looking at Tommy through the mirror.

"What if you could Like someone to death?" he asks.

VANITY OF VANITIES

"Earth Sucks" is written across Ken Roberts's Jeremy Scott crop-top. He's standing at the center sink in the girls' room of Willows High, sculpting his hair with Dippity-Do. He'd always coveted the center spot when Ken Hilton held rank. Ken Roberts has never looked so good, and that's saying something. It's like the glass has a built-in filter.

Ken Roberts's lips are especially massive this morning. He recently had Dr. Hilton blow them up. Ken Roberts has always considered himself the best-looking Ken. Of course, all the Kens claim they needed less surgery than the others, but Ken Roberts swears in his case it's true. He was born with a bitch face. A hospital room? He was expecting Fred Segal.

The stall door behind him is suddenly kicked open. Ken Roberts thought he was alone, but he isn't exactly surprised to see Blaine sitting on the top of the toilet, his boots resting on the seat. Big feet, Ken Roberts thinks as he appraises Blaine in the mirror.

"The glory hole is one stall over," he says. "But you have to wait until I'm finished doing my hair."

Blaine steps out of the stall and up behind Ken Roberts. Their eyes meet in the reflection.

"I want to offer my congratulations," Blaine says. "You've really come a long way from Ken Hilton's sidekick with a no-gag-reflex special feature."

"Ken Who?" Ken Roberts stares.

Blaine laughs. "I don't blame you for being jealous. Have you seen the Ken Hilton tribute videos on YouTube? A new one seems to pop up every couple of minutes. His least-viewed still has more than your top-viewed."

"Shut your peasant mouth!"

Ken Roberts frantically screws the lid back on his gel and says angrily, "Ken Hilton was a fraud. Did you know I wrote the lyrics to 'Hunty'? The melody came to me one day when we were having a kiki in Ken Hilton's bedroom. Ken Hilton's mom gave me a bump and it was like putting a coin in a juke-box. I just turned into, like, Superstar Barbie. Ken Hilton recorded me singing and dancing in front of the wall of mirrors, and then the next thing I knew, Ken Hilton demanded his dad buy him a recording studio and he and DJ Jazzie were recording together. 'Hunty' went viral and I didn't get so much as an acknowledgment, never mind royalties. Ken Hilton didn't even let me star in the music video. He said he only needed one love interest, and Ken Carson was cast. How embarrassing. *One* love interest. 'Zif that bih ever thought she ruled!"

"Ken Hilton was no dumb dummy," Blaine says. "He knew how to keep all eyes on him. And off the competition. I guess he'll always be more famous than you."

"Who can compete?" Ken Roberts asks. "He released his first sex tape when he was a Gerber baby."

"Not to mention, you're alive. Ken Hilton went from being a juicy story in life to a legend in death."

"Are you saying I have to kill myself to move as much product?"

"Not exactly. If you just kill yourself, Ken Hilton will still be the winner. He did it first. He's the OG."

Ken Roberts stomps his foot. "I could kill her for killing herself first!"

"There might be a way for you to be the star of the girl group," Blaine says over Ken Roberts's shoulder. "What if your death was getting views while you were still alive?"

"Now there's an idea I'd get a wrinkle for." Ken Roberts spins around to face Blaine. "How?"

"Think you have it in you to be the martyred twink?"

"I *love* a little bondage."

"You can make Ken Hilton's suicide seem superfluous. But it will require you to sacrifice your morals by pretending to actually want to help people."

"Then what will the help do?" Ken Roberts asks, sounding more genuinely concerned than he ever has in his life.

"You may not have a heart," Blaine says, "but other people do. At least, they like to use the heart emoji. If you want to reach a greater public than Ken Hilton, you have to appeal to more feeds. Ken Hilton's death started and ended with him. But what if you were the gift that kept on giving?"

Ken Roberts lights up. "Presents? I love presents."

"So you're ready to go live?"

VIDEO GIRL

Ken Carson raps Nicki Minaj's "Black Barbies" in the locker room shower after football practice. There are soapsuds in his ear when Todd calls him over to where he's sitting on the bench. Things are good between Ken Carson and Todd since their fight. Sometimes you just need to knock a guy's veneer out before you can move on.

"What's up, bruh?" Ken Carson rinses off and steps out of the shower.

"Have you seen this?" Todd asks.

He shows Ken Carson his phone. A tab is open to Ken Roberts's Facebook page. Ken Roberts's status says, "This will be my last post," and beneath is a countdown to a live stream.

"What's going down?" Todd asks.

"Don't have a clue, dude," Ken Carson says, drying off his balls with a towel.

Outside on the bleachers, two Stoner Conspiracy Theorists take rips out of a penis bong. One of them sees Ken Roberts's Facebook status and coughs out a lungful of smoke.

"Ken Roberts is about to post for the last time?" he croaks.

"I think this is in Revelation," his friend says. "Like, when Ken Roberts stops posting the beast is unleashed."

Everyone in the cafeteria is huddled over their phones, impatiently waiting for Ken Roberts's live stream to connect. What could it mean? A sense of dread percolates across tables, reaching the cheer squad in the center of the caf. They agitatedly sip their Diet Cokes.

Francie Fairchild's phone vibrates and she gasps. "Ken Roberts just texted me. It sounds like he's saying goodbye! He says, 'Tell the squad I love them and remind everyone that the biggest regret of women who have gotten breast implants is that they didn't go bigger xoxo.'"

The cheerleaders look at each other and try not to cry.

Allan comes up to Tommy at the lockers. He's holding out his phone.

"Okay, I'll admit it," he says. "I unblocked Ken Roberts

from Facebook because I'm curious. I was in the science lab and this is all anyone could talk about. Do you have any idea what it means?"

Tommy looks at the screen.

"It could be anything with that stunt queen."

Inside the girls' room, Ken Roberts stares down into a toilet bowl. He lets out a long sigh.

"Farewell, old friend. I showed you more than anyone else who I really am on the inside."

Ken Roberts closes the lid and climbs on top of it.

"Does my noose go with my shoes?" he asks, fastening the belt around his neck. It's attached to a pipe on the ceiling.

"Remember your lines?" Blaine asks.

"Of course. Breakfast is the most important meal."

"No, I mean what we talked about. You know what to say?"

Ken Roberts bobbles. "I've always been very oral."

"All right." Blaine lifts his phone. "Let's do this."

"Ew, not with that phone. Use mine. And bury me with it!"

Ken Roberts pulls out the pink-rhinestone iPhone from his pocket and logs onto Facebook. He passes the phone to Blaine.

"Catch me from my good side." Ken Roberts winks. "Pick one."

Blaine focuses the frame.

"We're live in five, four, three . . ." Blaine counts two, one with his fingers and points at Ken Roberts.

"Hai, bih, hai," Ken Roberts says into the camera. "So, I'm making this video for the entire LGBTMZ community. My heart literally breaks when I hear about gay kids being bullied or kicked out of their home because they're not accepted for who they are . . ."

Ken Carson and Todd hold each other as they watch Ken Roberts's live stream.

". . . homosexuality is criminalized in, like, hella countries," Ken Roberts says in the video.

The two Stoner Conspiracy Theorists watch Ken Roberts with red, bugged-out eyes.

"I just can't go on with my own perfect life knowing how many people aren't accepted," Ken Roberts is saying. "If I weren't so scared of scarring I would totally be sympathy cutting."

The cafeteria has gone quiet; the whole school is watching the live stream. Cries of sorrow from the cheerleaders of the damned.

"I hope that my death reaches people and makes them realize that #love, like, wins," Ken Roberts says. "Retweet me to heaven for a heaven on earth."

"I guess you could say I'm the younger, prettier Jesus." Ken Roberts's voice echoes out of Allan's phone. He and Tommy stare down at the screen with horror. "I died for you," Ken Roberts says, "so you could be free."

Ken Roberts blows the camera a kiss before stepping off the toilet seat. Surprisingly, his head doesn't pop right off.

Blond crown slumped forward, Ken Roberts swings in the stall.

Blaine lowers the iPhone.

"A star is born," he says. "To die."

HEIR HEAD

An early morning fog lifts off the streets of Willows Hills as Ken Carson goes for a run before Ken Roberts's funeral. His ass bounces in a pair of pink velour Juicy sweatpants.

Ken Carson can't believe his luck. He's so relieved that he doesn't have to play with Ken Hilton and Ken Roberts anymore. Ken Carson doesn't get it; they were at the top and they gave it up. For what? Ken Hilton because too much of everything is never enough, and Ken Roberts to be some kind of hero? Ken Carson wants to live! He wants to relish his popularity, not sacrifice it. What's the point of being famous if you aren't alive to experience the attention?

It's just so hilarious that everyone thinks Ken Roberts martyred himself because there isn't acceptance for gay people. Ken Roberts didn't believe in acceptance! He believed in exclusivity. If there was a moral behind his death it was that he was sick of living in a world where gay people aren't treated better than the "hetero peasants."

The headphones in Ken Carson's ears are playing music so loud ("Sexy and I Know It" on repeat) that Ken Carson doesn't hear the motorcycle driving behind him. The bike turns down Ken Carson's street and stops at the spiked wrought-iron gate of his house.

When Ken Carson jogs home, he stops in his tracks at the entrance. There's something sparkling on the ground.

His eyes bulge bigger than the bulge in his sweatpants.

The pink-rhinestone emblem of Ken!

Ken Carson picks up the iPhone and looks down the street to see who left it, but Blaine is long gone.

A red carpet lines the entrance leading into Famous Family Church. Barricades are set up to contain hundreds of onlookers, paparazzi and screaming fans.

Ken Roberts's head did pop off after all, and it rolled around the world. His Facebook live stream gets millions of views.

When Ken Carson arrives at the church, the crowd goes crazy for him. He stops to sign autographs and pose for selfies, and uses his new iPhone to take photos of his adoring public to post on SoFamous. The Tumblr has been getting more hits than ever before.

Inspired by his live-stream suicide, *Willows News* has decided to broadcast Ken Roberts's funeral live. Stacie Skipper stands next to the votive candles inside the church, smoking a cigarette and going over her script.

Ken Roberts's casket is cast in a single spotlight. He's dressed in his coronation regalia—Bob Mackie and a Cartier tiara.

Famous Family is packed. Everyone who isn't at the service is at home watching it on TV and crying into their popcorn—devastated they didn't get a seat (Ticketmaster sold out in minutes).

Tommy didn't try to get tickets. He goes over to Blaine's house to watch the shit-show live. He just couldn't bring himself to attend another funeral.

They watch as Dreamhouse diva Diana Wails greets mourners at the entrance of Famous Family by passing them vials of coke and a program to roll up and snort it with.

Stacie Skipper begins the service with a wide, white smile. "Good afternoon, I'm Stacie Skipper for *Willows News*, reporting from Famous Family Church at the funeral of seventeen-year-old Ken Roberts, the latest victim at Willows High School. Beginning tonight's sermon, Father Dude. Take it away, Padre!"

Father Dude walks up to the podium holding a crucifix in one hand and a tabloid in the other.

"The Bible may say suicide is a sin," he says. "But the *National Enquirer* says suicide is in."

The magazine features an article about Ken Roberts's suicide with the headline, "Death of an InstaStar!"

Willows News zooms in on Ken Roberts's corpse.

"Nice close-up!" Blaine leans forward on the couch and stares intently at the TV. "You can almost see the marks around his neck underneath the makeup."

Tommy squirms next to him.

Next, Stacie Skipper introduces Ken Carson, who reads

Ken Roberts's favorite poem—the lyrics to "Piece of Me" by Britney Spears.

Tommy has to look away. His eyes land on the end table where he spots Blaine's camera gun. The chamber is open . . .

Shit, I'm out of bullets.

Tommy grips the arm of the couch.

"Who do you think filmed Ken Roberts's suicide?" he asks.

TOY SOLDIERS

Fifteen-year-old Claude Christie from Emmett, Idaho, is the Kens' biggest fan. He has screenshots of all Ken Hilton's nude Snapchats saved on his computer.

For his school talent show, he performed the dance number from the "Hunty" video. It was totally worth the black eye he got afterward from the school quarterback.

Claude tries desperately to look like the Kens, but his school isn't as cool as Willows High; when he showed up for class wearing nothing but pink briefs he got sent home.

He bleaches his hair but can't afford to go to a salon, so he buys boxed dye from the drugstore. Unfortunately, it doesn't exactly match the Kens' signature shade. His hair is yellow and totally fried, but with the right filter it almost looks like a Ken helmet.

SoFamous.tumblr.com is refreshed by Claude all day every day. He gives each post a note, reblogging the Kens so much that his own Tumblr is basically a shrine.

The Kens are his greatest inspiration because they're so post-gay it's sickening. When Claude is being bullied by his cis-pig classmates, he doesn't let it get him down. He reminds himself that the Kens rule. And maybe one day he can too.

It's so touching that Ken Roberts killed himself to make the world a better place. Claude follows all the press. Ken Roberts is a sensation. Claude never thought in a million years that Ken Roberts would be more famous than Ken Hilton, but the bih did it! Ken Roberts is the patron saint of social media. Claude wants to be just like him.

So . . . he hatches a plan. He buys a gun from Walmart and gets his best friend to come over and record him as he commits suicide.

"Submit the video to SoFamous," Claude tells her. "I hope Ken Carson posts it! Wouldn't that be *everything*?"

Claude puts the barrel of the gun in his mouth and pulls the trigger. Blood and brains drip down the Zayn poster on his bedroom wall.

When Claude's suicide video appears on SoFamous, it causes even more of an uproar than Ken Roberts's live stream. Ken Carson posts the video using #KenSuicides. The hashtag takes off. Everyone shares the copycat suicide. Claude Christie breaks the internet. He proves that you don't have to be as skinny, glamorous or coked out as the Kens to get attention. Talk about a game changer. For the Kens' followers, this is their chance to shine.

Fourteen-year-old Johnny Skooter from Oregon raptures next. He steals his dad's car keys and turns on the ignition while the car is parked in the garage. As the garage fills with carbon monoxide, Johnny manages to take a final selfie and submit it to SoFamous. Ken Carson captions the post, "Savage as fuck! #KenSuicides."

It's on.

Sixteen-year-old Steven Tiff of Manhattan hangs himself in a Bergdorf Goodman dressing room. The sales associate records it and submits the video to SoFamous.

A small-town twelve-year-old Canadian boy named Kurt Darrin takes a selfie before killing himself by diving into his dad's ice-fishing hole.

Once the fever has crossed the border, it's only a matter of time before it crosses seas. International Ken! Buy on demand.

Bridge jumping, pill consuming, hair-dryer-in-bath electrocuting. New models coming to a store near you!

The videos, photos and obituaries of the #KenSuicides are featured on SoFamous. Anyone can grab a little glory. It's the biggest trend the Kens have ever started, even bigger than the Chanel ball-gag fad of '16.

It's, like, a phenomenon.

Jimmy Kimmel Live! airs a YouTube challenge video montage called "I Told My Kid Their Gay Sibling Committed Suicide," which sees devastated kids breaking down in even more epic fits of tears than in the videos where their parents tell them they ate all their Halloween candy. The studio audience laughs and laughs out of their seats.

The Kens' followers compete to see who can kill themselves in the most creative way. A photo of your slit wrists hanging over the edge of a bath filled with bloody water only gets half the notes of a time-lapsed video of you chugging a bottle of paraquat, for example.

Your death is only as successful as the number of clicks it

gets. No one counts how many actual people come to your funeral. They just view your Views and judge the value of your life accordingly. Obituaries consist of nothing but social media statistics.

The Willows High Stoner Conspiracy Theorists claim Ken Carson's campaign for teen suicide is eugenics. That he's been programmed by the Illuminaughty to help with population control. Ken Carson is preying on the superficial and mindless to get them to think that suicide is the most exclusive club to join. The theory picks up steam online. Ken Carson is reinvented as Ken: Cult Leader Edition. Scientology threatens to sue when it's reported one of the accessories that comes with him is an E-meter.

Along with the actual suicides, there are several fakes. Some followers are desperate to see the online reaction to their death but don't want to actually die, so they create content that makes them look like they've done the deed, submit the footage to SoFamous and bask in the mourning.

When Ken Carson gets tipped off that he's being duped, he has one of his minions check with the coroners in the city where the suicide allegedly took place. If you're found to be alive, everyone immediately unfollows you, and you're blocked from SoFamous. It's like you really did kill yourself, but without the glory—the most painful death of all.

ALL STAR

A week after Ken Roberts's funeral, Ken Carson hosts a #KenSuicides-themed party at Dreamhouse. Suicide videos from SoFamous are projected on the walls of the club and everyone is dressed to kill. Dreamhouse gives an open bar tab to the most dead-on dead look. It goes to Diana Wails, who's wearing a totaled Mercedes.

The next day, Ken Carson is booked for a sit-down interview with Stacie Skipper at the *Willows News* studio to discuss the Ken Suicides.

Ken Carson wakes up in the morning and realizes he passed out with his contacts in. Whenever he sleeps in them they make his eyes especially sore. He rolls out of bed, taking the contacts out before showering and getting ready for his close-up. His eyes are still irritated, so he decides not to put the contacts back in until right before the interview.

When he arrives at the studio, Ken Carson is more nervous than he's ever been. He's usually chill—some of the other Barks players get kind of anxious before a big game, but not Ken Carson. What does he have to be anxious about? It's not just the ball but the world in his hands.

He ducks into the studio bathroom to collect himself and put in his contacts. As he's standing in front of the mirror, a notification comes into his iPhone. Someone has submitted a post to SoFamous. Another Ken Suicide. Will it never end?

Ken Carson drops the phone in the sink. He doesn't even care when a pink rhinestone breaks off and falls down the drain. He takes his contacts out of their case.

All of these kids killing themselves in the name of Ken is really starting to get to him. Ken Carson doesn't want to encourage them anymore. That's it. He's going to stop—

The contacts slide into his eyes.

"Dude, you're so hot." Ken Carson winks at his own reflection.

What was he just on about?

Oh, yeah! Another suicide.

He picks up his phone from the sink and presses Play on the latest video. It's a Romeo and Romeo double suicide. One Ken wannabe drinks a vial of poison; the other shoots himself.

"Tubular!" Ken Carson exclaims. He posts the video to SoFamous.

His public demands it. They can't get enough. The Ken Suicides have made Ken Carson a legend. You can't buy this kind of publicity!

There's a knock on the bathroom door and a producer sticks his head in.

"We're ready for you on set, Ken," he says.

"Tight." Ken Carson bobbles. "I'll be right out."

Ken Carson turns to his reflection one last time, making sure his hair is perfect.

"You got this, bruh," he tells himself.

"Ken, you lost both of your best frenemies to teen suicide," Stacie Skipper says once the cameras have started rolling. "I can only imagine your pain."

Stacie passes Ken Carson a tissue for his nonexistent tears. He blots his lip gloss with it.

"The deaths of Ken Hilton and Ken Roberts have rocked Willows and incited a media whirlwind," Stacie continues. "There have been a string of copycat suicides across the U.S., being referred to as #KenSuicides. Is this an epidemic?"

Ken Carson flashes his diamond grills. "No one starts a trend like Ken."

"What do you say to your critics, who argue that you're promoting teen suicide by posting about the victims on your blog, SoFamous.tumblr.com, and, as a result, creating a contagion?"

"Hold up, bruh. I don't post *every* victim. No fats, femmes or Asians."

"What is the purpose of the Ken Suicides?" Stacie asks. "Is it political?"

"Um." Ken Carson scratches his head. "Yeah. Hella. You heard Ken Roberts. It's about, like, equality and shit."

"Isn't killing yourself for the right to live counterintuitive?"

"Socks with sandals is counterintuitive, Stacie. The Ken Suicides is the most influential gay protest since the Stonewall riots in the 1800s."

NETFLIX AND KILL

All week as the Ken Suicides are taking America by storm, Tommy can't bring himself to get out of bed. He tells his parents he's sick, and they let him miss school and even share their medicinal marijuana.

The truth is, he really is sick. With shame. The Ken Suicides movement started not with Ken Roberts, or even with Ken Hilton, but with . . . Blaine. And Tommy had been by his side every step of the way. He helped start the suicides, and he has no idea how to stop them.

Tommy keeps going over every detail in his head, trying to understand why he didn't see Blaine for who he really is. It's like Tommy transferred his desire to be a Ken into his desire for Blaine. He went from one illusion to another.

He periodically pulls his head out from under his pillow to scroll through the graveyard that has become SoFamous. Tommy keeps hoping that the site will load and he'll see that it's over. Ken Carson will have posted a video of his latest microblading appointment, and not another dead kid. But the suicides show no sign of slowing down.

Tutti is released from the hospital and returns to school. She and Allan get worried about Tommy missing so many classes and stop by his house to check on him.

Tommy wants so badly to tell them everything, but he can't bring himself to do it. What if he loses them? He just got himself back. He can't lose his friends now. He keeps up his sick-act and gets the feeling they don't buy it, but they're generous enough to play along. There isn't a single inconvenient truth in Willows. Tutti paints his nails, and Allan curls up in bed with him as they watch Netflix.

"What exactly is wrong with you?" Allan asks.

"Don't worry," Tommy says. "It's not fatal." But then he can't control himself and breaks down crying.

"Let's get these blinds open," Allan says quickly, getting out of bed and going over to Tommy's window. "Some sunlight might do you good."

"No." Tommy stops him. "Leave it."

Tommy knows he's acting weird. But if it's dark enough in his room, he can't see his reflection in the mirror.

"Blaine's been asking about you," Tutti says, like that might cheer him up.

Tommy has been ignoring Blaine's texts. Another reason why he doesn't want to go to school is to avoid seeing him. Right after Ken Roberts's live funeral was over, Tommy said he had to get home for dinner. "Don't want the kale to wilt." He tried to cover his shaking voice with a joke. Blaine offered to drive him home but Tommy said he'd rather walk. As soon as his feet hit the pavement, he started running.

"Did you see the latest Ken Suicide?" Allan asks, climbing back into bed with Tommy. "The kid was only ten years old."

Tommy closes his eyes. He's scared that on the night of his séance in Willows Forever Cemetery he really did invoke the devil. And now it's up to Tommy to banish him.

The next morning, Tommy shows up for school. He still isn't quite sure how to stop Blaine or the Ken Suicides, but he knows he can't keep hiding from them.

Principal Elliot has hung a selfie of Ken Roberts in the hallway outside of his office. Thanks to all of the publicity surrounding Ken Roberts's death, the school board has doubled Willows High's annual budget. School field trips are first-class to Ibiza!

Poor Ken Hilton. He's but a bad dream.

Students bring flowers to school and place them under the photo. There is such a huge pile that it spills into the hall and makes it practically impossible to get to class. Everyone has petals stuck under their sneakers.

Tommy kicks a bouquet of pink carnations. They scatter across the floor. He almost slips on a flower when he sees Blaine coming from the other end of the hallway.

"There he is," Blaine says as he approaches. "Why haven't you been answering my texts?"

Tommy finds himself backing against the lockers. Blaine

smirks at him, placing a hand on the locker next to Tommy's head and leaning in.

"There was another suicide this morning," he says. "All the way in Baltimore. Everyone's dying to be viral."

Tommy searches Blaine's eyes, hoping to see something that will tell him he's got it all wrong. Blaine stares right back at him, a small flicker of something in his eyes. But not remorse. Conceit, maybe.

"We were supposed to end the Kens' ridiculous trendsetting," Tommy says, "not reinforce it. Innocent people are dying!"

"Innocent?" Blaine forces a laugh. "The Kens' followers are not innocent." He touches the spot on Tommy's face where he used to have a scar. "What do you say we drive up to the peak tonight? Just you and me, alone, on a cliff . . ."

Tommy swallows. He doesn't let himself break eye contact.

"I thought you'd never ask," he says.

SHOWROOM DUMMIES

A big "Grand Opening" sign hangs across the front of Plastic Place. Hundreds of pink balloons are strung along the roof. The finished building looks as flawless as a hologram.

Shiny glass windows, shiny glass tile, shiny glass displays shining.

The boulevard surrounding the mall is paved with diamond-shaped mirror glass lit up with pink lights that reflect off the facade.

Plastic Place is opening tomorrow. All of Willows will be walking through its massive double-lacquered high-gloss doors.

For tonight, they're locked. But the side door is open. Pink light spills into the pitch-black basement.

There's shuffling, and a light switch is turned on inside the storage room.

Mannequins stop moving when observed.

Headlights brighten the back of the WILLOWSLAND sign. Blaine steps off his bike and looks around. The peak is dark and deserted.

"Come on," he says. "Where are you, Tommy?"

Blaine pulls out his phone and shoots Tommy a text. He had stopped by Tommy's house to pick him up for their date, but Tommy's mom told him he wasn't home. Blaine figured Tommy had already left. He hasn't lost the thirstiness that's made him the perfect play toy.

It's been a long time coming. For a while, Blaine thought he might be able to spare Tommy. He'd seen the error of his perfect ways and was even a good partner in crime. He'd rejected the Ken life—but that meant he was no longer clueless. Blaine can tell Tommy is starting to question his instruction manual.

The flapping page of a magazine on the ground catches Blaine's attention. He walks over to it, looking down at a copy of the *National Enquirer* open to the article about Ken Roberts's suicide. Blaine bends over and picks it up. There's handwriting on the top of the page.

The sun always shines on the internet.

Blaine smiles.

"You didn't," he says eagerly, looking around the peak.

Tommy isn't hanging from a branch on one of the trees . . . Maybe he did it on Kens' Trail? That would be poetic. Blaine moves to go and see, but stops when he notices a leg sticking out on the ledge beneath the peak.

He cranes his neck to get a better view, holding onto the trunk of a tree to stop himself from falling over.

Perfectly smooth skin, sculpted muscles, blond hair shining brighter than the stars in the sky . . . That's him, all right. The corpse is face-planted in the dirt, surrounded by a pool of blood.

"Tommy boy!" Blaine laughs. "I didn't think you had it in you. I came here to push you over the cliff, of course, but you went and took yourself off the market. You rocked the box and toppled off the shelf. Such a good little fame whore!"

Blaine leans against the tree, sighing as he stares out at luminescent Willows.

"Shame you won't be around for the grand opening of Plastic Place," he says into the sky. "There will be no returns for tomorrow's shoppers . . ." He pauses for a moment, and then goes on. "It's like Willows is the epicenter of the world's superficiality. And it's spreading . . . Just look at the Ken Suicides. The conveyor belt never stops; it keeps churning out product. It's up to me to put a wrench in the machine. Know how I'm going to do it? Won't Pops be proud . . . I only regret I won't be able to see his melting face. See, Tommy, tomorrow at the mall I'm going to contaminate the water system with acid and set off the fire alarm. The sprinklers will go off, and Willows won't be so pretty anymore."

"Hey, I just thought of something." Blaine kicks a rose-quartz rock off the side of the cliff with the tip of his boot. He doesn't hear it crack the porcelain below. "I'm kind of like a twisted older brother experimenting on his sister's dolls. This place is about to become a landfill."

MALIBU AVE

Across town, a camera crew is setting up on the front yard of Ken Carson's house. Tutti walks up the driveway carrying her makeup kit. Ken Carson told her to bring it. She was wary when the text came in, but he swore it was no joke and begged her to come over.

"I promise I'll explain everything, bruh," he wrote.

Tutti can't help but be curious. She's also cautious. Ken Carson has burned her in the past. Even if what Tommy told her about Ken Carson defending her honor after she attempted suicide is true, she still doesn't know if she can trust him.

When Tutti walks up the front steps of Ken Carson's house, the door opens before she even has a chance to ring the bell. Ken Carson pulls her inside.

He's shirtless, wearing nothing but a pair of Dsquared² shorts. Tutti doesn't know where to look.

"Dude, thanks for getting here so quickly." Ken Carson closes the door behind them. "You're into makeup, right? Ken Hilton would never admit it, but I know he followed your tutorials."

"He did?"

"Yeah, mang. You taught him how to *cunt*our."

Tutti laughs nervously and tucks a strand of hair behind her ear.

"Come up to my room, dude." Ken Carson leads the way.

They step into the bedroom and Tutti feels like she's in one of her dreams. Except it's even better because the smell is more intense than anything she could ever imagine. It smells like Ken Carson bathes in the water that drowned Narcissus and leaves ball-sweat fingerprints everywhere.

The room doesn't look like in her dreams. Tutti always thought the walls would be painted the same color as Dippity-Do, that there'd be a shag carpet on the floor, a glass ceiling and a revolving bed. But the decor is surprisingly minimal. There's a modern bed, and a Barcelona chair next to the window. Most surprising of all, there's a book on the chair, and as far as Tutti can tell, no white powder on the surface. Is that a *bookmark*?

Ken Carson peers behind the curtain on the window.

"So," Tutti asks, "do you want me to do your makeup for a shoot? Is that why there's a crew setting up outside?"

"Did anyone follow you?" Ken Carson faces her.

"I don't think so. Why?"

"How good are you at special effects?"

"What kind?"

"Puncture wounds, dude. I need it to look like I jumped from my window and landed on the fence spikes outside."

"What kind of video are you making, exactly?"

"Can I trust you?"

226

"Sure you can."

They sit on the edge of Ken Carson's bed, so close their legs are touching.

"I'm faking my death," he says. "The heat's on the Ken Suicides. The FBI is up on this shit. I think my phone is tapped . . . After my sit down with *Willows News* the police interviewed me. They think the Ken Suicides is promoting teen suicide and that it's, like, a cult. And I'm the leader dude because I've been *glorifying* the posts on my Tumblr. I have to get the hell out of Willows before they throw me in prison. I'll never survive jail. I'm the top Ken!"

"Well, you are kind of glorifying suicide by posting the Ken Suicides. It's like you're encouraging your followers to kill themselves."

"That's exactly what I said! When that little Claude Christie dude submitted his suicide vid to SoFamous, I didn't want to post it. But then Blaine met me down in the lockers . . ."

"Blaine?"

"Yeah, mang. I thought he wanted a piece—you know how it is. But he got all serious and started telling me how important it was for me to start using #KenSuicides and to blog any suicide posts. He said it was a way to honor Ken Roberts's message, to keep it going and, like, raise awareness for the oppressed during these tumultuous political times."

Tutti has never heard Ken Carson use such big words.

"Why don't you explain that to the FBI?" she asks. "You don't have to leave town."

227

"The truth is, bruh, I'm over it. Willows was chill, but now it's all stressful and shit. It's time for a rebrand. I think I'll try being, like, nice."

"But where will you go?"

"Back to Malibu. I'm going to make the waves pink. I hired a crew to record my death. Forget Ken Roberts: *my* suicide is going to break the internet. But I need your help."

Tutti's cheeks flush as she stares into Ken Carson's eyes.

"They aren't blue," she says. "You aren't wearing your Ken contacts."

"I hate those things," Ken Carson says. "They're scratchy as fuck. I only wore them because Ken Hilton made me."

"Maybe that's why you're different. Or at least, I thought you were . . . ." Her voice trails off.

Ken Carson puts his hand on Tutti's thigh.

"You know that video you sent me?" he asks.

"I'd rather forget."

"No way, bruh. I was, like, really impressed."

Ken Carson leans in and kisses her. Softly at first, until Tutti bites his lip . . . She can't help it! Ken Carson pulls back, bringing a finger to the blood. He breaks into a wide smile. When he kisses her again it's with such force that they fall back on the bed. Ken Carson pulls Tutti's panties off under her skirt. She balls the sheets in her fists.

When he looks up, Ken Carson has a shiny, proud smile.

"Dude," he says. "I could ride *this* pink wave all day."

UNBOXED

Willows is still. The moon shines its projector directly on Tommy as he walks down the quiet street. It all feels especially surreal tonight. The dolls' eyes are wide open and all-seeing, even when they're sleeping. There is no escape. All the alien toys that exist in other worlds have been put away on shelves and in boxes. A forgotten crayon lies on the carpeted floor next to a plastic dinosaur and awkwardly stacked blocks—on the verge of toppling over and crashing through the roof of the dollhouse like meteors from space.

Tommy enters the gate of Willows Forever Cemetery. He plucks a daisy from a grave and brings it to his nose. The porcelain flowers never wilt, but they also don't smell or sway in the breeze or feed bumblebees. They just exist, pretty little meaninglessness, always in bloom. If you grow accustomed to their artificial allure, you might start to believe you're meant to exist just as untarnished. But when you crush the petals into your hand you bleed. And unlike the tiny pieces of broken glass, you can be healed.

There's a shovel in the groundskeeper's shed. It clicks into Tommy's bloody palm.

Ken Hilton's grave isn't hard to find—there's a giant pink bow on the inverted-cross tombstone.

Tommy starts digging.

When he opens Ken Hilton's casket, the moonlight reflects off the cluster of diamonds on the corpse's face mask. Ken Hilton is perfectly preserved, his bronze arms eternally flexed. The pink-diamond stud remains in the one ear that didn't melt off in the explosion. Tommy lifts the mask to reach it. Curious, he pulls the mask all the way off.

Ken: Picasso Edition. Ken Hilton's eyelashes are fused together, and one eye droops down onto his busted cheek implant. His face is all burnt skin and melted collagen. There are only a few platinum-blond strands left on his scalp.

It's like all of the ugliness within came out of the holes in his head and enveloped him.

Tommy takes off the pink-diamond earring and rolls it between his fingers.

It slides into his ear painlessly.

Taking cover under a fake plastic tree next to the stairwell, Tommy watches as hoards of people walk through the front doors for the grand opening of Plastic Place.

The mall reeks like the floors were washed with Sour Puss and mopped dry with cotton candy.

A beaming blonde-bimbo saleslady stands at the entrance of a department store, spraying a sample bottle of perfume.

"Life is your creation," she coos to passersby.

The water fountain in the center of the mall is spraying in sync to "Barbie Girl," which is playing through the mall speakers on repeat.

Barks players and cheerleaders pass Tommy. Todd is vaping and blowing the smoke through a bubble wand. Bubbles float over heads and into stores where they pop, releasing tiny twisters of smoke.

A photo booth never stops taking pictures. The flashing bulb is pulsating as fast as Tommy's heartbeat. He looks up at the ceiling, trying to count fire sprinklers.

Screaming.

There's a life-sized dollhouse around the corner where kids are playing.

It's so crowded Tommy almost misses Allan and Tutti as they shuffle past.

He grabs the handle of Tutti's cosmetics shopping bag, pulling her and Allan behind the tree.

"Tommy!" Tutti exclaims. "I was hoping you'd be here. Did you see Ken Carson's suicide video?"

"Ken Carson killed himself?"

"It was just posted," Allan says. "What are you doing behind a tree?"

"It deserves an Oscar," Tutti says, reaching into her purse and pulling out the Kens' pink-rhinestone iPhone.

"Where did you get it?" Tommy asks as Tutti passes him the phone.

"Ken Carson gave it to me." Tutti can't meet Tommy's eyes. "He told me to give it to you."

"Why would he want Tommy to have it?" Allan asks.

"I guess you're the closest thing to a Ken left in Willows." Tutti shrugs.

"There might not be a Willows as we know it for much longer. Have you guys seen Blaine?"

"I saw his bike in the parking lot," Allan says.

"The side door . . . ," Tommy mutters to himself. "Allan, if someone were to contaminate the mall water system, how would they do it? Through the pipes in the basement?"

"Possibly. But a building this size might have its own water tower, which would be located on the roof."

"The roof!" Tommy is about to run for it, but Allan steps in front of him.

"What's going on?"

"You know those chemicals that went missing from the science lab at school? I think Blaine is the one who took them."

Tommy leaves Allan and Tutti to try to evacuate shoppers from the mall *without* ringing the fire alarm. He darts to the top floor, running down the hallway where Blaine took him the first night they visited the Plastic Place construction site. Tommy bursts through the door. His eyes screw up from the blinding sun, and he spots Blaine on top of the water tower.

Blaine is dumping a container of acid into the water. Even from below, Tommy can tell the water is reacting violently—

steaming, boiling and foaming over the side of the tower.

He hasn't been noticed. Tommy ducks behind the water tower and pulls out the "camera" gun he surreptitiously took from Blaine's house while they were watching Ken Roberts's funeral. After running into Blaine at school, Tommy bought bullets from a kid in the caf capitalizing off the Ken Suicides. He climbs the ladder to the platform on top of the water tower, and points the gun at the back of Blaine's head.

"Strike a pose, bitch," Tommy says.

Surprise makes Blaine drop the acid. It rolls off the top of the tower and spills across the roof. Tommy is relieved—but there's a second container next to Blaine's feet.

"Well, well, well." Blaine slowly turns around, staring through the barrel of the gun. "Aren't you supposed to be dead?"

"My head like a mannequin."

"You faked your death with a dummy?" Blaine crackles. "Nice! But why'd you trick me, Tommy? I thought we were closer than that."

"Were we ever, really? Or was it all in my head like everything else? I was always in my head dreaming about being a Ken, and then I was in my head dreaming of killing them. Were you all in my head too?"

"Let's just say you were the tear in the packaging. Because of you, the Kens made themselves vulnerable."

"You sick fuck!"

The gun shakes in Tommy's hand.

"Were the Ken Suicides your plan all along?"

"Who can predict what will fly off the shelf?"

Blaine unscrews the second container of acid and begins pouring it into the tank. The exothermic reaction is even more intense than with the first batch: the water convulses, hissing with each drop. Tommy's eyes burn from the fumes.

"I'll shoot," he says. "I swear I'll shoot!"

"No, you won't. You never really had it in you. It was just so easy to wind you up."

Blaine empties the container and tosses it over the side of the tower. At the same time, a balloon attached to the roof comes loose, floating above them into the sky. They hear it pop.

"It has to be done," Blaine says. "There's no end to the Kens' influence! It's not just school, or Willows: it's the whole country—all of the Kens' followers, everyone who has ever used #KenSuicides. We're not just living life through the filter of a screen, we *are* the screen. It's spreading, coating people. Coating families . . . Don't you see, Tommy? Plastic Place has to burn to remind the world how to feel."

"I won't let you do it!" Tommy closes his eyes and squeezes the trigger. "Not this time."

"Tommy!" Allan pushes through the rooftop door.

The sound of Allan's voice makes Tommy release the trigger. He opens his eyes just as Blaine swings at him. The gun is knocked out of his hand; it lands on the roof and spins. Tommy almost falls with it, but manages to grab onto the side of the ladder just in time. Blaine's quickly on him—he wraps his hands around Tommy's neck.

"Where's your reset button?" he says through gritted teeth.

Tommy swings at Blaine, hitting him in the nose. Blaine stumbles back, bringing a hand to the blood gushing from his nostrils. He smirks.

"I expected more from you, Tommy. I thought you were, like, woke," Blaine says mockingly. "But you never managed to completely deprogram from Ken Hilton's handiwork. It's up to me to break the screen."

Blaine grabs Tommy's arm and drags him toward the water.

"You're just as bad as the Kens." Tommy desperately pulls away. "You're not doing this because you care about changing the superficial world; you're doing it because you want people to think you broke the mold. It doesn't matter what you want to be known for. You still want to be known!"

Tommy manages to reach into his pocket and pull out the iPhone Tutti gave him. He lifts it in the air.

From below, Allan yells. "It's over, Blaine!"

Allan slips in spilled acid as he fires a shot with the gun.

Simultaneously, Tommy brings the pink-rhinestone iPhone crashing down on Blaine's head.

Glittering pink particles rain down into the water, landing on the surface with a spark. The phone crumples to dust in Tommy's hand. He imagines the Kens in their caskets doing the same. Poof! *Plastic just gets smaller and smaller.*

From the shock of being hit by the phone, Blaine releases his grip on Tommy. The blast from the gun blows Tommy into Blaine, pushing them toward the opening of the tank. Tommy steadies himself, but Blaine loses his footing. He rocks back on the heels of his boots, flailing his arms and desperately reaching for Tommy's hands. Tommy blows

Blaine a kiss—and as the sticky sweet doll breath hits him in the face, Blaine is knocked into the water.

He makes a single, ear-splitting scream. And then nothing.

Allan drops the gun next to the acid containers and rushes up the ladder. He appears next to Tommy out of breath; he pulls out his inhaler and takes a huff. He and Tommy slowly lean over the opening of the water tower and peer inside.

Blaine has completely dissolved.

All that remains is his leather jacket, floating on the surface.

"You're bleeding!" Allan gasps and points at Tommy's chest.

Tommy looks down. Blood is soaking through his shirt. He's been shot.

"'Zif," he says, right before collapsing in Allan's arms.

WE'RE JUST GETTING STARTED

Brown roots are starting to show in Tommy's blond hair. He needs to redo his eyelash implants, and he's in desperate need of a shot of Botox. The past few weeks have been harsh. His lips look as blown up as they did the day he stepped out of the factory, but eventually they'll lose their luster. He's considering asking his mom and dad for plastic surgery for Christmas. They rushed to the hospital when they found out Tommy had been shot, tipping off Stacie Skipper for an exclusive along the way. Tommy just won't tell them that he wants the surgery to reverse some of the procedures Dr. Hilton performed on him. Maybe he can get featured on an episode of *Botched* with Barbie Hilton!

Tommy wants all his implants taken out—butt, cheek, chin and his pecs, even if they did save his life. The bullet Allan fired trying to stop Blaine from throwing Tommy into the water tower lodged in Tommy's left pectoral. The silicone shielded him. The most damage done was to Allan's "Parked in a Parallel Universe" graphic tee, which got covered in Tommy's blood.

Allan carried Tommy from the water tank into the mall, down the elevator and into the parking lot. He didn't stop running once, his glasses slipping down his nose with sweat. By some kind of miracle, Allan's car made it all the way to the hospital without breaking down.

On the way, Allan called the Willows Police Department and told them about the contaminated water. The mall was shut down over a suspected terrorist attack. Tutti had managed to hustle a few people out earlier by telling them Ken Hilton had been resurrected on the peak. She'd been inspired by a photo a group of hikers posted to social media of the mannequin Tommy used to trick Blaine. Tommy left it up there, along with the empty bottle of ketchup that served as fake blood. Works every time.

For once, Tommy is glad for the shameless digital extensions he calls parents and agrees to give *Willows News* an exclusive.

He tells all of Willows the truth about the Ken Suicides, including the role he played. The WPD interview him right after the *Willows News* broadcast, but Tommy is off the hook—in part because of mall surveillance footage, which shows him trying to stop Blaine from contaminating the water system. He also suspects it's because he's an eyewitness to what the police did to Brad. Tommy gets the feeling they want to avoid more bad publicity than they've already suffered. As usual, it all comes down to image.

It dawns on Tommy that his parents, like other citizens of Willows, need to be superficial to survive. As soon as you start questioning your reality, it unravels, and most people would rather have a red carpet under their feet than wrapped around them so tightly they can't breathe. He decides to accept his parents for who they are. Not as brave as him. Once you've seen through the mannequin matrix you can never be blinded by beauty again.

Tommy doesn't expect Willows to change overnight, and the truth is, he doesn't really want it to. Not everything has to be taken so seriously. Despite its flawless flaws, Willows has some redeemable qualities. It's a place where life really is your creation—anything is possible if you believe in it. He just hopes that enough people learn something from the Ken Suicides—enough to start believing in something more than rock-hard abs. Like maybe in themselves.

The doctor tells Tommy he's lucky to be alive; without the protection of his implant, the bullet would have struck his heart. The idea that his heart might have been stopped by a bullet reminds Tommy that he has one, that he doesn't have a disco ball rotating in his chest like a Ken. He has a real live beating heart and it's the accessory that goes with everything.

Once he's healed, Tommy will have a small scar from where the bullet struck his chest, but other than that, he's coming out unscathed. He's actually looking forward to having a scar again. As he glides his finger across his plumped cheek where his old scar used to be, he thinks of the feeling of his finger swiping across the screen of his phone. Blaine wasn't totally wrong; it was just his methods that were demented. Maybe the screen *is* spreading, and a little crack—not enough to break you, just enough to remind you that you can be broken, isn't such a bad thing after all.

So one day he'll wither and decay and eventually disappear and won't be an eternally mint-condition object of envy and glamour. No one said life is fair. The truth is, there is a glamour to changing, to eventually losing everything. There is a great glamour in disappearing. There's the great beyond. Or be-lond, as a Ken might say. The uncertainty of it all is the most outrageous, shocking, gag-worthy headline ever written, because you can't read it until you're dead.

A week after being released from the hospital Tommy is up in his room listening to "Hunty" in honor of SoFamous being wiped from the internet. The Stoner Conspiracy Theorists claim it was seized by the FBI, or perhaps by Baphomet himself. Tommy's just glad to see it go. Maybe the students of Willows High don't need to be led.

It doesn't take long for a new blog to pop up in its place. FuckYeahTutti.tumblr.com is followed by everyone. It's a page dedicated to Tutti's makeup photos and tutorials. Tutti plays coy when she stops by his house to visit during his recovery and Tommy asks who she thinks made it. But by the way she smiles to herself, Tommy gets the impression she knows exactly who her number one fan is.

From the foot of the stairs, Tommy's mom yells up at him. "Turn that music down! You know I have celiac." Tommy rolls his eyes. She has no idea what that means. Long before Blaine tried dumping the acid, there must've been something in the water in Willows. Maybe he'll make it past the wall one day and see what the real world is like.

There's a honking outside his window. Tommy turns down the music and looks outside. He goes rigid.

It can't be . . .

Parked in his driveway is Ken Hilton's pink Corvette. It honks again and Allan jumps out, waving up at Tommy's window.

"What the—"

Tommy runs down the stairs and out the front door.

"Allan?" he says, stepping onto the driveway.

"Hey, Tommy." Allan smiles.

"What are you doing with Ken Hilton's Corvette?"

"Dr. Hilton sold it to me. I've been saving up my Taco Accessory paychecks to buy a new car. My old one's pretty much kaput."

Tommy laughs. "You don't say. But why this car?"

"Okay, I'll admit—I secretly always liked it. Even when the Kens were trying to run me over. Wanna go for a spin?"

The WILLOWSLAND sign stretches across the hills. The dollhouses beyond are framed by the back of the giant letters.

Tommy and Allan are sitting on the hood of the Corvette. The sunset is pink. Another day is coming to an end in Willows. It's bath time then lights out for its young god.

"Is that Ken Hilton's earring?" Allan touches Tommy's ear.

"I kind of robbed his grave . . ."

Tommy takes the earring out and stares at it between his fingers. The glow of the sunset reflects off the stone's jagged edges.

"I knew I had to stop Blaine. I thought if I wore Ken Hilton's earring that maybe some of his confidence would rub off on me. He wore it with the pride of a crown jewel. It was symbolic of his superiority and ultimate power—"

Allan takes the earring from Tommy's hand and throws it through the center of the O. It disappears in the pink haze.

"You never needed it. Ken Hilton didn't help you stop the Ken Suicides. It was all you, Tommy."

"I guess it had to be. I did start them, whether I intended to or not."

"I hear Plastic Place may never reopen," Allan says. "They closed it to make sure the water was clean, but the safety inspector discovered Blaine's dad had defied a ton of zoning laws and didn't get the right permits."

"Maybe he'll sell it," Tommy says, "and Willows can get its first mosque. Some diversity might be all this place needs to take it outside of itself."

The peak begins to cool as the sun slips beneath the hills. Tommy shivers and Allan removes the red flannel sweater he's wearing over his T-shirt, wrapping it around Tommy's shoulders.

"I'm surprised you still want to be my friend after everything I've put you through," Tommy says. "You warned me from the start not to become a Ken."

"I just wish you had come to me sooner," Allan says. "Like right after Ken Hilton died. But it wasn't your fault, and in the end, you did the right thing. I thought it was really brave that you went on *Willows News* to tell everyone the truth."

"Well, I wasn't totally innocent. Hanging out with Blaine made the Kens look like they were manufactured for pre-schoolers."

Tommy lets out a long sigh.

"I miss him," he says.

"Are you kidding me?" Allan jumps off the hood of the car. "What was it with that guy?!"

"I mean, I miss the idea of him. I thought Blaine liked me before I transformed into a Ken. I'll never find that out now. Even if I do reverse some of my plastic surgery, I'll never be me again. Everyone who meets me will see a Ken."

"Not everyone," Allan says, climbing back onto the hood. He lifts his eyes to meet Tommy's. His cheeks are as flaming as his hair.

Tommy stares into Allan's eyes, clinging to the sweater around his shoulders. It smells like fast-food grease and lab chemicals. Beats leather. Tommy's safe. "I guess I was so obsessed with how things could be, how I thought they *had* to be for me to be happy, that I didn't see what was right in front of my old face," he says. "I didn't see that there was already happiness, if I only chose it."

Tommy reaches for Allan's hand. "Why didn't you tell me?" he asks.

"You always made it seem like anything less than the Kens wasn't worthy. Maybe I was worried I didn't measure up."

243

"You'll have to forgive me." Tommy squeezes Allan's hand. "I wasn't thinking."

He almost holds his breath but doesn't let himself this time. Tommy wants to feel this. He closes his eyes, leaning in to kiss Allan, and—

it's *perfect*.

THE, LIKE, ACKNOWLEDGMENTS

TY Westwood Creative Artists—Liz Culotti who helped me create the perfect shade of pink, and my daddy, Michael Levine.

TY Lynne Missen, Margot Blankier, Linda Pruessen and Erin Kern at Penguin Random House Canada for being the Hocho, Eyes and Ribbon emojis to this text.

TY Five Seventeen, Anthony Gerace and Chris Howey for putting together my very own Barbie box.

TY Daniel Waters and Tina Fey. In some parallel universe I'm still showing up to school and getting a right hook to the nose for acting like a Heather Chandler/Regina George hybrid. The Kens were born of the blood.

TY Literarische Colloquium Berlin where some of this book was written.

TY to my family for their support and cabin on Lake Winnipeg where some of this book was written.

TY Susan Safyan, Suzanne Sutherland and Liz Levine for insights on my pretty mess.

TY torsos of Grindr for all the inspiration.

TY Jaik Puppyteeth for your tattoo designs, one of which I gave Blaine.

TY Quotewise for curating Ruth Handler quotes.

TY Mattel for the big dreams not sold separately.

RAZIEL REID is the author of *When Everything Feels Like the Movies*, which won the 2014 Governor General's Award for Young People's Literature and has been optioned for film. He lives in his head, which is based in Vancouver. Follow him @razielreid.